For the Grandchildren

Tír na nÓg

Áine's Diary

By Nancy Chambers

Editing and Pictures
By Philip Ward

ISBN: 978-1-907107-28-3

A CIP catalogue for this book is available from the National Library.

This book was published in cooperation with
Choice Publishing & Book Services Ltd, Drogheda, Co Louth, Ireland
Tel: 041 9841551 Email: info@choicepublishing.ie
www.choicepublishing.ie

Acknowledgements and Thanks

My thanks are due to all those who have helped in any way to make this book possible.

Particular thanks are owed to:-

Peter Beirne at the Clare Studies Centre, who has been so helpful and encouraging from the outset,

Austen Hobbs of the Clare Champion for taking time to discuss old photographs and hunting in the archives,

Nicky and Gerry Considine for additional information when needed, and for their wonderful hospitality. Also for providing 'The Robin' poem, written by Gerry's Aunt Catherine at the age of ninety,

Sandra Sandland for proof reading the manuscript and offering helpful comments. Also for overall encouragement at all times.

Carrie and Alan for being my inspiration.

My grateful thanks to Philip, without whom this book would not have been written.

CONTENTS

"Where glows the Irish hearth with peat,
There lives a subtle spell–
The faint blue smoke, the gentle heat,
The moorland odours tell
Of long roads running through a red
Untamed unfurrowed land,
With curlews keening overhead,
And streams on either hand;
Black turf-banks crowned with whispering sedge,
And black bog-pools below;
While dry stone walls or ragged ledge
Leads on, to meet the glow.
From cottage doors that lure us in
From rainy western skies,
To seek the friendly warmth within,
The simple talk and wise."

'Poems we learned at School'
By The Fireside by T.W. Rollaston

CHAPTER 1
WHY AM I HERE AND IS THIS WHERE I BELONG?

There are two people standing on the shore; the younger asks, '*Where did it all begin?*'

They are at the water's edge absorbed; one thinking, '*I can look forward but I cannot see the future, therefore it doesn't help me,*' the other thinking, '*I can look back and see the past, but I cannot change anything, therefore it doesn't help me.*' The first has his life ahead of him, but what does it hold? The second believes that life is almost over, but what does the remainder hold, and how will knowledge of the past help?

The elder is focused and concerned for the younger and his journey into the future. As they stand watching the waves breaking gently over their feet, on the horizon can be seen a passing ship, coming from who knows where, and bound for some unknown distant land.

The younger says, '*If I were aboard that ship where would it take me?*'

The elder replies, '*I don't know what its destination is, or where the vessel is bound, but we can be sure that she will be sea worthy and equipped to deal with all eventualities, the storms and the calms of a deep ocean crossing. Similarly on the journey of life we must be prepared - not anxious- but ready.*'

'*How can we be prepared,*' the younger asks, '*and what should we be ready for?*'

'*Well, we live on in the memory of those who love us: our legacy, the legacy of our ancestors, and the legacy of our faith. Life can be very inconvenient you know, taking care. For example, it can be very inconvenient when we need to take care of nature and the environment, and to take care of each other. We need to consider the value of nature, and human nature, and the beauty of both. Not everything and not everyone is immediately at our disposal. We cannot order life through our whims, and our whims cannot dictate our journey. We come from a deeper level, where our agendas are different, giving rise to compassion, but also to those things which are lacking.'*

Looking at the younger with a gentle smile, the elder says, *'I cannot tell you about your journey, because I cannot see the future. I can though, try to tell you about some of my own experiences, and I can tell you about my grandfather, who taught me to be a good listener, and helped me to develop a philosophical and caring outlook; and the importance of discipline. I would like especially to tell you about the first nine years of my life after my dad, mum and brothers landed on my grandparents, to share their home, in a place so special that I never really wanted to grow old - I didn't even want to grow up. You know, it's not difficult, all these years later, to imagine what life would have been like for them; having settled down to comfortable retirement, with a live-in servant for my grandmother, and farm help for my grandfather, when necessary. They had their own social life, and enjoyed visiting friends and having friends to dine with them, and share many a long chat. But with the arrival of two parents, two older boys, one infant girl and one younger brother on the way, life was never going to be the same again.*

The world was at war then, and even in what was a very remote place, the restrictions caused by that war were felt over a period of time, and blackout material always had to be readily available. The result of all the shortages, coupled with fear and rumour, was to add to the hardship suffered by local farmers, particularly those who had no other means of financial support.

Many people visited my grandparents to share their worries: listen to the radio for news up-dates and, as always, to have a cup of tea, a glass of sherry, a dram or two, or a bottle of Guinness. By the time they were leaving, the sombre mood had vanished and they seemed to be in much better spirits, even though some of it was of the liquid variety! After such visits the mood would change again, when my grandfather would share his concerns for some of our local friends, with my parents. Although there was an abundance of natural beauty in this part of The Burren, the land itself was very poor and difficult to cultivate, making the table feast a triumph over adversity.

In my home there were other problems too. My grandparents dispensed with their outside help, and my father and mother undertook the tasks of running a home, and coping with a very large family. There was no electricity or running water. At times it was a very heavy burden for my mother, who had not experienced these shortages before. We, as children, were expected to be the extra hands and feet, wherever and whenever we were needed, but because we knew no different, we were happy to do so. The boys were often out-of-doors, helping or playing, and when allowed I took off with them; it was usually possible to pop outside to stand and gaze in wonder at the scene before me. My thoughts were free to roam and there was time to remember, and sometimes to recall the words of a hymn from the previous Sunday. One of my favourites on such occasions was:

Holy God, we praise thy name;
Lord of all, we bow before thee!
All on earth thy sceptre own,
All in heaven above adore thee.
Infinite thy vast domain,
Everlasting is thy reign.

My grandmother had a very upright stature and, with a typically Victorian approach, was always concerned with the 'do's and don'ts' of living. She had been a French governess for a time, and had taught with my grandfather before marrying him and starting a family. She always looked very smart and serene, except first thing in the morning! She sometimes made porridge, which the children weren't keen to eat, and who would be when it was made of porridge oats, water and salt! This was when the milk had run out, and the cows had not yet been milked, and there was no choice, merely a lot of reluctance and a wish that this was something which could be passed on to the dog. We could never understand what grown-ups saw in that type of porridge, but they seemed to enjoy it! Grandma would hover until the bowls were clean, and we would be sent to get ready for school, vowing 'never again'- at least until the following morning when, hopefully there wouldn't have been too many visitors the evening before helping to use up all the milk. There was usually sweetened condensed milk available, but this was kept for tea, in emergencies, and anyway it didn't flow round the porridge very well, even when it was allowed. We were always reminded that this was good food and others would be very glad of it – no doubt, but it didn't make it any easier to get it down, but because grandmother's health was failing we needed to be on our best behaviour.

My grandfather was always kind and very thoughtful where others were concerned; he was what you would call an upright individual. On one occasion he took me with him when he visited the new headmaster of his old school. While sitting on Grandfather's knee as they chatted, I heard them say that it was a pity that they couldn't have had daughters, because my Grandfather had four sons and the new Headmaster also had boys. Much to my disgust I heard them say, 'How could she be such a tomboy, with so many beautiful curls!' Well, I think they were teasing me, but didn't they know that I didn't want the curls, because I was so unhappy when Grandmother brushed my hair from my neck upwards, which dragged all the delicate hairs on my neck and brought tears to my eyes; also I wanted with all my heart to be able to wear trousers in order to keep up with the boys. They didn't fall off walls because their knees had got stuck in a skirt! The final indignity was being told, 'Well you're just a girl after all!' I could only listen when the two men spoke, but had to forgive them, because they couldn't know what it was like to wear a skirt, and I couldn't interrupt their conversation!

While speaking, the elder found that the years had rolled back as though they had never been, and she experienced all the joy of being a nine year old girl again ....

.... Asking too many questions will always get me into hot water, but I am prepared to bother whoever happens to be available because I need to know. Asking where I have come from usually gets the standard answer. If I happen to be sitting on Father's knee the answer is gentle but is always, The Stork! Heavens, don't they know that they have told me that one at least half a dozen times before, and don't they realise that living on a dairy farm leaves little to the imagination. I need to know why, if I was born in Dublin, I am now living in Ballinalacken, County Clare. One is on the east coast and the other on the west coast, and there are a lot of miles in between. Because life is difficult and everybody has to work very hard, there isn't time for what are considered to be unimportant questions, and busybodies often get short shrift with an answer such as, 'Not now', or 'When you are older', or whatever comes to mind. That is alright and I am used to it, but it always remains on my mind until the next time. After all, Grandfather is always saying, 'Try and try again'.

Gradually, however, I can begin to piece things together, and when we have local visitors or when my relatives come from Dublin to visit us, I am quietly present and 'all ears', until they notice I am still there!

The house I live in was built for my grandfather when he became headmaster of the local school, and it was there that my father and uncles lived until they were old enough to go to Blackrock Boarding College in Dublin. After College they found employment there; getting married eventually and settling down with their own families.

At the outbreak of war, families with young children were advised to move to the country, if that were possible. My father chose to bring his family to Clare to live with my grandparents. Because I was an infant at the time of the move, I wasn't aware of the impact it would have on the family, and I couldn't make comparisons, but as I grew I often wondered what it might have been like living in a city instead of this place, which is described as being 'out in the sticks'. There is no electricity in Ballinalacken nor is there any running water. I wonder too how different it might have been if my two older sisters had survived their infancy and were here to share with me. Well, at least they would have to wear skirts as I do - what an imposition!

Because of the move my father no longer has regular employment, and this increases the financial burden on my grandparents, but there is always plenty to do on the farm. In addition, there is the impact of the war, with luxuries few and far between, but what do they mean by luxuries? We children have never known such things so we never miss them.

The house, which is called 'Rockville', was built with its three side windows facing the sea; these are kitchen, main bedroom and dining room windows, all having a clear view of the ocean and the distant horizon. The building appears to be on the same level as the distant Cliffs of Moher, which are approximately nine hundred feet high, and they take the full force of the worst of the Atlantic gales. The house is surrounded on all sides by an escallonia and fuchsia hedge, which leaves the kitchen window exposed because this faces the drive and side path. The main drive continues round the side and into the yard at the back, where there are some outbuildings. From there a number of steps lead up to what is called the high garden, where vegetables are grown and where the peat and potatoes are stored over the winter. The path leads round the front to the other side, which is the main entrance, and by the path there is a small kitchen garden, which is divided from the small front lawn by a low privet hedge. Below the windows, at the front, there is a narrow border where irises, stocks and monbretia flourish through June, July and August. The main vegetable garden is some distance from the house and form part of the farm itself. My brothers and I are not confined to our small garden because, for our playground, we have the freedom of the countryside and are happy to make full use of it. The view from the windows is an ever changing, magical, mystical scene, except when there is a need to close the shutters in order to keep out the full force of the gale, and then we just stay indoors!

This evening, now that the table has been laid for dinner, there seems no more for me to do in the kitchen. Needing time to dream I take myself outside and stand gazing at the scene before me, whilst trying to recall the poem we have been learning at school, and which needs to be 'off by heart' for tomorrow morning. Oh, what a jumble of thoughts are going on in my head, as my gaze travels down over the fields and the stone walls towards the sea, where the waves are splashing on the shore. This only happens when the tide is full and the sea very rough, but I so wish I could be closer because big waves always take my imagination in a different direction. Well, I must be satisfied with viewing from afar and finish learning this poem.

The Fairies
(A Child's Song)

Up the airy mountain
Down the rushing glen
We daren't go a-hunting
For fear of little men;
Wee folk, good folk
Trooping all together
Green jacket, red cap
And white owl's feather.

Down along the rocky shore
Some make their home
They live on crispy pancakes
Of yellow tide-foam;
Some in the reeds
Of the black mountain lake
With frogs for their watch-dogs
All night awake.
By the craggy hillside
Through the mosses bare

They have planted thorn-trees
For pleasure here and there.
Is any man so daring
As dig them up in spite
He shall find their sharpest thorns
In his bed at night.

Up the airy mountain
Down the rushy glen
We daren't go a-hunting
For fear of little men
Wee folk, good folk
Trooping all together
Green jacket, red cap
And white owl's feather

(William Allingham in Favourite Poems we Learned in School by Thomas F. Walsh)

'Down along the rocky shore, some make their home' is my favourite line, but I can't be down there now and I don't want to think of goblins, dragons, leprechauns or any other little people because I am not much bigger myself. I want to think about the flower fairies which are my favourites!

It isn't a problem trying to imagine beautiful fairies because we have lots of pictures of angels in church, in school and in our little Mass books. So, if angels are from Heaven can there not be a higher place, because my flower fairy images are even more beautiful than the angels, but they are so difficult to describe? They have such delicate faces and bodies, with dresses made of gossamer silk and in every colour of the rainbow too. They have wings that look like the dewy cobwebs which appear on the trees in the autumn, still covered with dew drops. They move so daintily as they waive their tiny wands and hover over the plants and the flowers which they tend, and of course they love to play with the butterflies. We are told that they live at the bottom of the garden, using toadstools to shelter from the rain and sun. We are told too, that each of us has a Fairy Godmother, and I hope that mine is as nice as those I have imagined!

With the exception of the Fairy Godmother, I know that all else is make-believe, but this place where I am standing is very real. As I take in the beautiful scene, which always excites me whatever the weather, I become aware that someone is standing behind me, and turning I see my grandfather, who has been sent to tell me that dinner is now ready. I don't know how long he has been standing there but he understands that 'wandering off' is not being moody, as my brothers have said, but just a need to understand some things, sometimes.

'Oh Granddad, can I ask a question? Why can't my eyes see what my imagination sees?'

'Well my child, you will have to pretend that your eyes are like our old box camera; when you look through the lens you can only see so much of the whole scene. You look through the window, and you focus on the scene you want, click the shutter to capture that image, and only then can you move on to the next part of the scene. When all the pictures are printed you can put them together and you will have this beautiful panorama that your eyes can only see in stages.'

'Oh, that was good, is there time for another question?'

'Only if you're quick!'

'When I am grown, will I be able to explain things as you do?' Just then a voice comes from the open kitchen window, announcing that dinner will be cold. Oh no, now we're both in trouble and it's my fault again! He takes my hand and as we go indoors he says, *'You will be able to explain many things when you are older, but you will never be able to describe all the beauty you see here, because words alone are not always sufficient and a person needs to be here. Beauty is an individual and personal thing; we don't just see it, we feel it deep inside because it feeds our senses, but only the creator knows how His creativity really works.'*

'Yes, I know about the creator Granddad, but can you tell me about senses?' We have already arrived indoors, where the silence speaks volumes. Oh dear, but it has been good! I have mixed feelings because I feel that there is a lot of sadness in

Granddad these days, when he thinks no one is noticing, and I sense that this is because my grandmother is often confined to bed. I will think about it tomorrow on my way back from school.

CHAPTER 2
THE BOX CAMERA

The road to school, which is about a quarter of a mile or so from home, doesn't have too many distractions. The land is uneven with many little dips, but there are different shades of browns and greens made up of rushes, thistles, grasses and mosses, which vary in intensity throughout the year. The odd bush and boulder are too far apart to make much difference, and it all looks a bit bare.

A gentle climb takes the road past two farmhouses and their outbuildings, where it meanders down the hill, along the bottom and climbs the other side past the school and on until it disappears from view, and there seems little to notice but the sky itself; the school stands stark and grey against the bareness. The journey home, however, is always very different.

Learning how to look through a lens has been very exciting, and today is going to be full of experiment, but it will have to be on my way home. Once out of school it is difficult to resist the temptation to remove my socks and shoes, and this has to be the first thing I do. Oh, what a sense of freedom, and then the tingling sensation throughout my body, while treading carefully on the uneven gritty surface. Practice has taught me how to put my feet down lightly, so that if a stone is too sharp my foot will arch itself and the weight will be transferred to a different part; it is easy to move onto the grass verge, if there is a need to for any reason, and most of this journey is on the grass.

It isn't a road for daydreaming, as it passes by one particular farm, where the 'sow' lives, but that's another story. I am remembering now what Granddad has said about using the camera. He has explained how to focus, and today I must put it into practice. I don't usually notice the scenery about me, as I leave school and set out for home, but today is different. There is such a feeling of excitement while walking down the hill, along the hollow and up the other side, hurrying past the farms, with no time to even think about the sow. Thankfully she sleeps in the afternoon. It is here where the road rises to its highest point that everything changes. The contrast is so unbelievable and a backward glance is necessary for reassurance. The adults have often said that seeing is believing, but it is so, so difficult to take it all in on this beautiful day. This scene of wonder which speaks to me silently, seems to send messages in and through me; my heart wants to sing but isn't able. There is peace and a certain stillness; there is a feeling of space and timelessness, with the silence being broken only by the singing of the birds and the humming of the bees. With my feet now resting on a soft grassy patch, I am conscious of being part of the earth beneath my feet, and the sky which is above, and all around me. For a moment it seems unreal, but I am listening and looking, and remembering the words that my grandfather has spoken, 'a person needs to *be* here'.

Well, this is *being* here, and being part of all Creation, but there is a feeling of *belonging* too, and with this understanding comes that peace and stillness. Then I realise that these moments are all about my inner journey, but what about the outer journey, and the pictures, and what about that other sensation which is becoming more persistent! Oh, my big toe; never mind the toe now, must look at the pictures.

I am standing in the centre of the narrow road, looking straight ahead, focussing through the imaginary lens and making my own mental picture. What can I see? There are wide verges on either side with a covering of grass, weeds, thistles and nettles. The road is a mixture of different greys but they are not as interesting as the stone walls which enclose the fields on either side. Every stone is a different shape and colour, but together they make up the walls which, even though they are meant to be straight, have a slightly rambling appearance, but manage to remain standing, except at one point where the stones have given way under their own weight and now lie in a heap on the verge. The road ahead disappears and a tee junction is formed at the bottom, where on the left-hand corner, surrounded by escallonia and fuchsia and with only the chimneys and top of its roof showing, sits my home. Beyond and below this is the Atlantic Ocean with, on the left hand side, a distant view of the Aran Islands and, on the right a view of the Connemara Hills on the horizon. The sea is a mixture of blues and greys, varying in intensity, but seeming to reflect the colour of the sky, which has a mystical blueness, broken by a number of wispy clouds. There is no sun to make the water sparkle today, but the sea is calm and helps to create a very peaceful picture.

Turning to my left, while refocusing the camera, provides a very different scene; where beyond the first field the bareness disappears giving way to many shrubs and pasture land. It is easy to see the Castle ruins surrounded by trees, where my brothers and I often spend many hours climbing in order to reach the top and declare that, 'We are monarchs of all we survey'. From the top we have an excellent view of the Cliffs of Moher, but I don't need to focus on them today because I have them in the picture frame of my mind. A turn to the right and I focus on the meadow and fields, which form part of our farm, and where I have spent some very happy hours.

Having captured a lovely panoramic image in my mind, I skip the remainder of the journey home, arriving indoors where my grandmother is waiting for a report on what I have been 'doing in school today'.

CHAPTER 3
THE MEADOW AND CHURCH

The meadow is such an important part of my life, since it is there that I seem to be able to examine the 'Why, Which, Where and How' of things; and although I can't often find all the answers, as grown-ups aren't always available to help me with my questions, it somehow seems sufficient to be able to accept 'what is' and still be happy.

The feelings and emotions that are part of my being are just 'heart and mind'. I don't think about how things came to be, they simply are, and all of nature's wonderful provision seems to be for my pleasure; but it also has a profound affect on the way I look at, and accept, adult behaviour. Nature's provision is bountiful and I have been endowed with a very lively imagination, which sometimes causes a problem when I need to explain myself. My parents often say, *'Where did you get that idea from?'* I simply retreat within myself, storing up my ideas until others are able to understand. But whatever they think, this is my imaginary world, where I soak up all the natural beauty around me: the shapes, the colours, the climate and all its moods, and the taste and touch of all that is available. It is not difficult to recall my parents or grandparents comments, when I appear before them having fallen in the nettles, yet again, *'If you gently touch a nettle it will sting you for your pains; grasp it like a piece of metal and soft as silk remains.'* Those words sound strong and make me feel good inside, but they don't ease the pain in my arms and legs. I am told to go back to the meadow to collect some dandelions; not just the heads, as I might wish to, but the stalks as well; because this is the part which I should squeeze and rub on my stings and it always works. Oh, the joy when the weals begin to subside and the pain eases. As I return to my world with all it's discoveries, I wonder why it is, that my grown-ups, who are very intelligent – I know because others have said so - cannot see the pictures I create when I see the clouds, or even when I accidentally get red berry juice on my white blouse; the colour is so beautiful and will look lovely as little red spots all over the garment - or so I imagine. Then there was a particular occasion when I felt I needed to disappear to my imaginary world - to one of my favourite places.

There were few family arguments in my home, but on this occasion I sensed that I could be a nuisance if I remained in the room, and I decided to slip away to the meadow, when no one was looking. Although the clouds were gathering the sun was still shining, and I liked to lie in the long grass and look at the clouds or the animals or just pick the daisies. But I had forgotten that my Grandfather had bought a few sheep, and a lamb had appeared a few days earlier. I had never been so close to sheep before, but I had watched the lambs in the distance, in springtime, skipping and playing, totally oblivious. But this was very different. A little lamb was so close that I could see her tight curly coat and four spindly, wobbly legs. Her bleating cry sounded very feeble. I watched her wobble away from her mother, and again that pitiful cry, because she was too far away from her mother, who was unperturbed and continued grazing. Eventually though, she had to wobble back for reassurance. It had started to rain, but I was so engrossed in this scene that I hadn't noticed; then it was raining very heavily and I saw a flash of lightening and heard the thunder. I knew I should rush home but I couldn't leave the lamb looking so dejected, so I gathered her up in my arms and together we found a hollow in the wide stone wall and waited. The storm passed quickly and I left the lamb close to her mother. Going back indoors, feeling very happy with myself because, although I was very wet, the lamb's coat was only damp. When my parents saw me looking dishevelled but happy, they were at first relieved but then very angry because they had been worried. Oh, and I thought I was being protective because I didn't want the lamb to suffer, and they had not told me that the lamb's coat was waterproof.

The lamb had touched my emotions in a gentle protective way, but I was also deeply touched whenever I saw and heard the skylark, although in a very different way. This is the bird that taught me about Glory, and what Heaven could be like, because I associated Heaven with what I always felt was a gift from God; this bird that could fill my heart with her sense of being. I used to sit quietly in a meadow and watch the skylark rise from her nest in the grass, and as it rose it started to sing, this to distract attention from her nesting place. The singing would become louder and more beautiful, as it climbed up through the clouds, upwards and onwards until I could no longer see the tiny form, but could still hear her song. I always felt a deep emotion and a sense of fear; this tiny bird must soon explode with the intensity and volume of her song, but the emotion was really a sharing of that same intensity, as my heart soared with it, until I thought that my own heart would not cope any more. Then came the sadness when I could no longer hear this heavenly sound, and felt that perhaps the bird had gone to Heaven itself and left me behind. In the quiet as I gazed upwards, I realized that the little form was descending, swiftly, silently and very peacefully, to land unnoticed in her nest. I felt a sense of peace and joy knowing that she was back with me. The bird and her nest were so perfectly camouflaged that, in order to find it, one had to move very gingerly, and the best time to do this was when the skylark was high in the sky. Then it was possible to find the nest in the long grass and count the eggs being hatched, usually three or four.

The lamb had been my first lesson in bewilderment; being protective towards one of God's creatures, as my parents said I should be, had got me into trouble. Then there was the joyful association with the skylark, where I was only an observer. Life, that wonderful teacher, seemed to be telling me that these two go hand in hand.

I often journey out alone, but there are occasions when my three brothers and I are sent on errands, when we cross the fields to reach our destination. These are mini voyages of discovery, as we travel further and further, which is a delight to me but my dalliance often frustrates my brothers, and they have no time for my daydreams. On such occasions my eldest brother's face turns red with frustration, because he has to wait around, since he is responsible for us youngsters. I feel sad that I have been the cause of his impatience, but on one occasion he uttered loudly, *'You know the bull is just over there behind those bushes, so I would get a move on if I were you'.* This galvanised me and the daydreams were put aside until we reached a point of safety, when a quick look at my brother's grinning face showed me that this time it had merely been a ploy; but I could never ignore such a reminder again, because there are bulls on the farms, and since they are known to be bad-tempered, we ignore advice at our peril.

This is a time when children are to be seen but not heard; we are told to listen and pay attention to our elders – out of respect – in the home, at school, in church and in the community, we always have to obey. Listening is mostly easy, but obeying is another matter altogether; at least for me because I have my own thoughts and ideas which, for the most part, need to be contained. We are never allowed to interrupt an adult's conversation, and the opinions of children are not considered to be important. When adults gather children are expected to be well behaved, speaking only when they are spoken to, and asking to be excused but only if it is really necessary; those are the rules.

So far I have lived in a very remote part of The Burren, where there are no cars or telephones, so visits from friends are very rarely pre-arranged, folk simply turn up; they may have walked for miles, used a bicycle or a pony and trap, but they are always made to feel welcome. If it is just one visitor there is never a problem, because the rule at mealtime is to lay an extra place at the table 'just in case', and the meal is shared and stretched. There is always tea and rich fruit cake as a standby, and because we children are allowed to share the cake it is a rare treat. Regardless of the number of visitors, and as soon as we have eaten, my brothers excuse themselves quickly on some 'urgent' pretext; anyway it is generally accepted that the boys will naturally prefer to be out-of-doors. This general adult opinion is very difficult to accept, particularly as they all agree that I should have been born a boy, since my behaviour is so tomboyish; but can they not understand that, with only brothers as playmates, I have to play their games and four is an ideal number for so many children's activities, especially where pairs are involved.

On these social occasions it is not a problem for me to stay behind, as listening is very entertaining, and there are many funny stories told; some about people I know and some about others whom I don't know but try to imagine. There is talk about living, socially and politically – most of which goes over my head. I enjoy the adult tone and remain attentive until the mood becomes sombre; and there are muted whispers behind the hand, when I ask to be excused and go away and think about this strange behaviour!

Paying attention in church is never a problem, and Sundays and Holy Days are always welcome. I know that God loves me; I am special to Him, and His Son appears in the crib each Christmas. He, like me, has once been small and that makes all the difference. It is so easy to relate to Him in this way, and I feel thankful that the One who has created all the natural and beautiful things, which I love, has also created an infant who grew to be an adult, as I expect to be one day – whatever that really means; but my heart is full of love and thanks, because now it is possible to understand that here is my invisible friend, who will always know how things are with me; and it doesn't really matter any longer that the grown-ups can't see my imaginary pictures.

Mass normally involves one server and the Priest, who always seems a bit remote, because for most of the celebration he has his back to the congregation, and speaks in a language which many of us don't understand. When he reads the Epistle and the Gospel he turns to face the people, and it is possible to have a closer look at him and hear what he is saying. When he reads the Epistle, and speaks about God's wrath and fiery nature, I don't understand – it just feels so uncomfortable – and I am always so much happier when he reads the Gospel, because the words have a different tone, and the stories have a simple message that is easier to understand, even when they seem to say that the people are not always as nice or as good as they should be. But I know these stories are about Jesus, the Son, who is my invisible companion, and I feel a little put out when the reading says 'follow me', because it doesn't seem possible to follow someone who is already so close. As the tone of the stories change throughout the year, it is difficult to understand why He needed to die just to prove that He loved me. Thinking about it seems to cause a feeling of pain, but at the same time joy, which is again difficult to understand. But this strangeness that I feel doesn't last too long, because being the sort of person I am, my imagination can always take off in any direction.

On one occasion, while listening to a reading which described the transfiguration of Jesus, and how his face 'shone like the sun, and his garments became white as light', I found myself distracted with imaginary pictures, but was brought back to earth quickly on hearing the words, 'He was still speaking, when lo, a bright cloud overshadowed them, and a voice from the cloud, said, "This is my beloved Son, in whom I am well pleased; hear him.". Oh well, that's it then, I thought, 'I cannot see God the Father; cannot even imagine what he would be like, but I know what His Son is like, and this is His Father speaking to him from a cloud; but if He could create the world, He could surely speak from a cloud!'.

My journey home from Mass on that occasion was one of the happiest memories. The clouds now have a new meaning, and they are no longer merely a source of fun, providing hours of entertainment, as my brothers and I try to describe what their shapes remind us of.

CHAPTER 4
THE PEAT BOG

Providing fuel to keep the home fires burning, as well as stoking the range for cooking is a major occupation which starts about the end of April. Nobody is really happy about the prospect of setting out on these expeditions, least of all my Father, who has suffered a lifelong battle with rheumatism from the age of twelve, and knows from past experience that this exercise usually results in days spent in bed; the working days are long and the work is back-breaking.

With a promise of some fine, dry weather, we duly set out. 'Getting ready' is a major event in itself and unless my brothers or I are ill we are expected to help at this time. Mother, who remains at home to cook and look after my grandmother, always prepares lots of sandwiches and makes tea, which is put in stone bottles and wrapped with strips of woollen material to keep the heat in. There is always sweet soda bread with sultanas or raisins for afters or later in the day. Father has to collect the pony from the fields; harness it and attach it to the cart, which has the creel fitted for this journey. The creel is rather like a slatted play-pen which can be fitted to the cart when needed, and on this occasion it is necessary because everything we will use for the day's work has to be carried with us.

When 'the children' are ready they remain out of sight until such time as Father says, *'On your marks, I need everyone who is coming to be in the cart in five minutes.'* Oh, this is fine for my brothers who have long legs, and spend more time climbing trees than I do, but I'm not being left behind - the outdoors is calling. My brothers usually stand inside the cart laughing at my feeble attempts to scale the creel, and the struggle usually continues until Father appears and hoists me over the top – Oh, the indignity; being an eight-year-old girl who has to wear a skirt is no fun.

Once we are on our way everyone becomes light-hearted. It is very pleasant jogging along in the cart, feeling the heat of the sun on our faces and remembering stories or just gazing quietly at the landscape, which is just showing signs of spring. In no time! Well, in about half an hour, but it depends on the co-operation of the driver and pony, we arrive at a place where we have to leave the main road to join the track which leads into the bog. At this point Father says, *'All out!'*, and we climb out of the creel. He unloads the equipment: releases the pony, unharnesses it and tethers it to the cart or a large boulder, so that it can remain grazing until we return later in the day. Each one of us has a bundle to carry. Father pushes or pulls the peat barrow, made out of wood with a wooden wheel, and carries cutting equipment. We walk the remaining distance which is about half a mile; wishing, much of the time, that our bank was a little closer to the road. It all looks very flat and uninteresting, except that this is one of those places where the song of the skylark will lift our spirits. Who can count the most skylarks and not fall into the ditch whilst looking upwards! Well, we won't go there right now because I am the one who usually falls in. We arrive at our bank eventually; the question is why this place and why do we need to come here? Well, that question can probably wait until we stop to have our drink.

Later, when we stop for a break and we all sit down to drink our tea, Father gives us a lecture about how the peat bog was formed.

'It was a long time ago – thousands of years in fact – there were many thick forests here but our ancient ancestors decided to clear the trees to make way for pasture. Without the trees, the quality of the soil changed over time, and the grass gave way to rough growth such as heather and rushes. The roots of this scrub didn't break down and were left behind to form a substance which became very springy and wet because the drainage was very poor; this was called peat. There were certain areas where the drainage was better and suitable for harvesting the peat, and this is one of those areas. For generations past each family has had its own bank in this

bogland and from here enough turf is dug to supply the family's heating needs for twelve months. And now it's back to work or you may have to stay here all night!' Oh Lord, with Will-o'-the-Wisps and Jack-o'-the Lanterns, but I can work as hard as my brothers anytime. Father has said that peat is decomposed matter in water and partly carbonised. Well, a lot needs to happen before it will look like the pieces Mother feeds into the range.

Father is the only person strong enough to clear the surface, using a very sharp-edged spade, or slicer, in order to get rid of rough heather and grass roots. These surface scraws, as they are called, are either pitched to the bottom of the bank, which is usually water logged, where they make a firm base; or they are tossed to one side on the bank. He needs to dig to a depth of about one foot before reaching the first usable turf; this looks brown with lots of stringy bits and, when used in the fire, it burns too quickly but it is perfect for starting fires – especially when it has some paraffin oil or candle wax added to it. The best turf is at the bottom; it looks more like coal but is wetter and heavier to lift than the brown. Once the surface is ready he uses a turf-cutter or *sleán* to slice straight downwards and lift the sod of turf onto the bank; the *sleán* is a special piece of equipment which looks like a narrow spade with a sloping ear that allows a rectangular sod of turf to be cut, measuring about twelve inches by four inches by three inches. The sods, which have a lot of water in them, are lifted carefully into the peat barrow. Father works quickly and it isn't long before the barrow is full. At this time my eldest brother will drive it a distance from the cutting area and tip it onto a rough patch. The remaining children are on standby to take these sods and lay them on the rough ground. Everyone works in harmony, and there is a lot of chatter until lunch time approaches, when the talking ceases and the silence indicates that we are all hungry and it is time to stop for food. The sandwiches taste like manna from Heaven but the tea, which has lost some of its heat, has developed a taste all of its own and we children prefer to have spring water or milk, which are the other options.

While eating we are able to look around and see where other families are working; indeed there are a number who, like us, have taken advantage of the beautiful spring day to get it all started. By now the sun is high in the sky and there is a gentle breeze moving the rushes; and those stems which I have spotted on the way in, when there was no time to dally, could now be inspected. There are lots of little tufts or mounds round about and each mound has a number of single stems growing there. Examining them more closely I find that the seedheads are almost ready to open. I know that when we come back in a few weeks time the heads will be a mass of white, and this plant which is called bog cotton or cotton grass, thrives in this boggy soil. Each head of cotton when it opens has masses of short snow-white strands that feel so soft and delicate to the touch. Oh, I will have to ask Mum when I reach home what we can use them for because surely we can use them for something. But now I can see that I am the only one not working since I have wandered away from the others; oh dear, will that mean having to stay behind! Perhaps they hadn't noticed yet!

This is a long day and we have worked well into the afternoon, but now it is time for a drink and some cake before we prepare to leave and return home. We trudge back across the path, to be re-united with the pony which has grazed lazily through the day. We are so thankful for the cart ride on the return journey. We know that there will be at least two more journeys before all the turf will have been cut, but we cannot think about what we will be doing next, because just now it is so good to smell the peat smoke as we near home, knowing that Mum has a hot meal waiting for us.

There are two further trips to complete the cutting, but on these occasions I may be busy helping Mum in the house. This means going to the spring to collect water for tea-making, which is always a struggle. I wonder why nobody has thought of making buckets with short handles for little people, especially since this seems to be a chore for the children.

The weather has remained warm and sunny, which is ideal for drying the turf, and about two weeks after the first cutting we set out again. This will not be such a difficult day because the turf just needs to be turned; 'many hands make light work', we are told, and so we spend the day completing the task but with breaks for drinks and a chance to really enjoy the scene around us.

There are few plants to enjoy when we first visit the bogland, although there is a feeling of promise because spring is definitely in the air, and the song of the skylarks seems to be everywhere. This journey is so different and the change is a lesson on one of nature's miracles. The heathers, lichens, mosses and grasses have all felt the rays of the sun, and start to offer up their myriad shapes and colours; a feast for the eyes. But the icing on this glorious natural cake is the bog cotton which has fully opened to reveal its tufts of white elegance. The other name occasionally used to describe this grass is hare's-tail cotton grass, and this suits my image when I survey it. It looks like thousands of hares, nose down, tail up and bobbing about in the breeze. I can feel the silkiness of each, and I am lost until I hear a voice say, *'We might have to leave her behind'*. Oh no, they have finished while I have been daydreaming and are now preparing to go home. They are not angry though because they and I knew that we children won't want to come next time.

The next visit depends very much on the weather; if there has been too much rain the sods become water-logged underneath and they will need to be turned again. If it has remained fine over the two-week period a dry crust will have formed and they are ready for the next stage. We are lucky, because the sun has been shining each day and the breeze has been strong. My brothers try to find excuses, and I am seriously thinking of having stomach ache, but this will result in a dose of 'the dreaded castor oil' for anyone with sudden pains, and that stops me in my tracks.

On this occasion we won't need any tools just our hands because it is the 'footing' stage; there is quite an art to this footing business since it involves standing four sods upright in a lean-to manner - like an Indian teepee - and then placing another sod on top. Oh, fine, there is nothing to it really particularly since Father makes it look so easy, but doesn't he know that small hands have short fingers! Taking one hard-crusted sod with two hands and placing it firmly in an upright position is so easy; take one hand away to reach the second sod and the first starts to slide slowly back to it's starting point – and this is only the first one.

Working at our own pace, we labour through the day trying not to notice our aching backs. The brown turf is not too difficult to handle because the fibres don't become too hard, but the black turf is a better fuel and there is a lot more of it. We have more breaks for drinks on this occasion, and it is good to straighten up, but my, isn't it painful whilst picking the sultanas out of the soda bread in order to eat them separately. Maybe it is a reminder that this isn't how it is supposed to be eaten! Regardless of the aches, it is still a joy to see the change that is taking place around us. The colours are deepening more plants are appearing and the sight of all the little stacks of turf belonging to different families, is a joy to behold with the sun reflecting on them. What a lot of teepees – if only the little Indians could do the work, our fingers wouldn't look so red.

Since there has been very little rain it is possible, two weeks later on, to go back to the turf scene taking with us: the pony and cart, the donkey and panniers (side baskets which sit astride the donkey's back), and what looks like a wooden sledge, with a raised surround, which has been made by Father. This is attached to the pony's harness, using two special chains with a bar to separate them. Our task is to fill the panniers and load the sledge with sods. Filling the panniers isn't a problem as we can simply toss the sods in and then pile some more on top. The sledge is more of a problem because the edges need to be straight in order to achieve a bigger load. Fiddle-de-dee, wouldn't it be easier to have panniers on the pony or have another donkey, but this definitely isn't a day for questions! All our energy is needed to transport the turf from the bank to the roadside and there unload it, taking home with us the last load, having transferred the turf from the sledge to the cart. But, what about us! Sitting atop the load doesn't bear thinking about and anyway what about the poor animals. Well, we don't need to be coaxed to sleep at the end of the day. The rest of the turf will have to wait until we can move it in stages and stack it near the house.

CHAPTER 5
GOING HUNTING

Going hunting is always a very special expedition because it's Dad who takes us and for a while we are out of Mother's way. Sometimes all of my brothers will come too but that depends on what else they are doing. Of course I am happiest when they are all doing other things, because being the sort of inquisitive person I am, I have a much better chance of asking my Dad questions, and it is more difficult to concentrate if we are all there. As he is always hopeful that he will be able to bring a rabbit home for Mum, there is usually an air of tension when we go hunting.

There is as a rule, on every occasion, the instruction, *'When I say quiet I mean now!'* We all know what that means, since our dinner might depend on our good behaviour, so we try to do our best to behave. There is a strict rule too, on no account to touch the gun, because we could lose an arm or a leg, kill ourselves, or even worse kill someone else. But what about the rabbit – one minute he is bobbing along with his little white tail going up and down without a care in the world, not yet having picked up the scent of the dogs or sensed any danger. In an instant all that will change. We will have our orders to fall into line until such time as the aim is taken, the gun discharged and the rabbit seen to drop. The dogs are ordered to, *'Go and get it!'* Then it becomes noisy again and the boys can lark about, but I have very mixed feelings until Dad reassures me that the aim was good and it has not suffered. Generally we return home with a few rabbits, and sometimes a hare, but since the hares seem to be able to outrun the rabbits there aren't too many of those.

The ideal environment for hunting is when the weather is a bit hazy, as often happens in the summer after a rainy spell, because the rabbits will have remained sheltered and then begin to appear slowly, whilst all the time sniffing the air, but it is difficult for them to pick up a scent in these conditions because the atmosphere is still moist.

The best area for hunting near our home is the scrubland, where there are lots of shrubs, hedges, mounds of thistles and rushes, and, of course, nettles. The rabbits thrive there, and they build their burrows everywhere. Occasionally even one of the dogs gets carried away when it decides to chase a rabbit and follow it all the way into its burrow. It is a funny sight seeing the dog with its head stuck down the burrow, where it remains until Father finds it and yanks it out.

While the sound of the discharging gun may have bagged a dinner, it also alerts the other rabbits, as well as the grazing animals, which includes the bull, but Father is usually very careful. On one occasion, however, he had misjudged the distance so that when we heard him whisper - in a tone we had never heard him use before – *'when I say run I want you to run straight to that wall over there, and climb as fast as you can without looking back'*. We waited and then did as ordered. Having scaled the wall we knew that we were safe now to look round, but only to see the bull closing in on Father. Oh dear, we have heard of people we know being gored by a bull, and there was a feeling of real terror because we were so helpless, just watching; only my invisible friend could hear my plea! Dad was safe, but only just, and the bull pawed the ground near the wall as it bellowed in anger and frustration. One rabbit, on that occasion, was more than sufficient!!

CHAPTER 6
THE PIG

Running the farm didn't include keeping pigs, but pork was part of our diet and very useful during the winter months when rabbits and fish weren't so easily available.

So it was, that when the harvesting was finished, I heard my grandfather say one morning, *'So-and-so is bringing the pig this morning, and so-and so and so-and-so are coming this afternoon!!'* Oh my life, not again, this is just too much but where can I go; not to the meadow, that's too near, and I can't go too far because they will worry and it will just be double pain! In that case I had better think about tomorrow and pretend that today isn't happening.

Just as promised, the man and the pig turned up in the middle of the morning, and I went out with my grandfather to have a look. There was a lot of general talking in the yard, and then it was down to business as they bartered over the price, but eventually they shook hands and money was handed over. The man left but the pig remained – that day I didn't want any lunch. I had to have stomach ache, because if I forced the food down then surely I would have problems later. I even felt sick just thinking about the afternoon. Soon after lunch the butchers arrived, and then I quietly disappeared to my bed-room, where I waited for the first squeal before burying my head under the pillows. Even then I could still hear the noise. Later, when it was quiet, I could find my mum in the kitchen and ask if 'that bit' was over. She would say '*Yes, and next year would be different because the pig wouldn't suffer'*, as she dried my tears. It would be different because the butchers would have humane instruments. But today there is such a lot of work to do, because apart from the pig's unusable offal the other parts will need attention. The carcase is cleaned, washed and hung inside the outer door of the back porch; this is unfortunate for me because I can't help thinking that it might just hop down and chase me, like that horrible sow that lives up the road, but that's another tale.

The most important task, after the pig-slaughter, is to use the blood as quickly as possible because we don't have a fridge. Watching Mum prepare the black pudding mixture is quite an experience; she uses oatmeal, fat, onion, and pepper to add to the blood; it is the men's task to thoroughly clean the intestines and soak them in salt water for a time, before being filled with the pudding mixture. The real art is in tying one end, before filling, and then the second, and completing the process by tying both ends together to create a round shape which is better for fitting into the pot, because the puddings need to be boiled for a time before they are ready to be used.

The word usually spreads – not that words are necessary because I think the squeals will have been heard over a wide distance. In the evening some friends come to join us. The ribs have already been removed from the carcase and are cooking in the oven. The puddings have cooled sufficiently to be cut into slices and fried. My brothers and I have been despatched to bed because it has been a long day and the adults are tired too. But who can sleep with all those wonderful cooking smells, and who will be the first to be spotted at the kitchen door; and how will Dad and Mum re-act. There is only one way to find out and it is worth the effort, because then our hunger will be satisfied and anyway the spare ribs are delicious with brown soda bread. I will leave the black pudding to the adults.

Some days later one butcher returns to cut the carcase into joints, which will then be pickled for a time before being hung on the kitchen ceiling, to be used when needed, but it never tastes quite like the spare ribs on the first night.

CHAPTER 7
AS THE CROW FLIES

One of the many highlights of the summer holidays is the annual visit of Uncle Ben and Aunt Alice, who come from Dublin, and stay for two weeks in a hotel in Lisdoonvarna. They are both teachers and have a long summer break, spending some time at home and then visiting other relatives before coming on to visit us in Clare. They are always relaxed and happy, being full of fun and, much to my delight, are available to answer some of my many questions. Aunt Alice is an infant teacher and well equipped to cope with young minds!

For weeks before they arrive I learn to contain myself in the hope that there will be answers to my questions. Of course, this is the busiest time of the year in my home and on the farm; no one will appreciate my endless harassment and as the visitors often eat with us, my mother has many preparations to make. With regard to the food there is little that she can do in advance, except make fruit cakes, which store well but need to be hidden because everyone likes fruit cake, particularly my eldest brother. Fresh salad is available from the kitchen garden, and vegetables from the main garden some distance from the house. By this time the bacon which was cured last autumn has almost run out, and Father doesn't really have time to hunt or fish, but if possible he will go to Caher on an occasional Thursday evening, to fish for herring or mackerel, because we don't eat meat on Friday. The main alternatives are chicken – oh no, one of my pets – or lamb chops, or mutton.

Joining my uncle and aunt for afternoon tea at the hotel is always a special treat and, weather permitting, we are able to eat outside on the lawn and enjoy the music, which drifts up from the Spa Wells, as there is music and dancing there out-of-doors in the main summer season. I love the atmosphere and I am always eager to go there. Seeing my eagerness my aunt says, *'Hey, it's only a hop, skip and a jump, and we'll be there later.'*

When they first arrive I still need to be very patient for a few days, because they spend so much time chatting with the family over endless cups of tea. They always have their lunch with us on the day following their arrival, because my uncle needs time with my grandparents. This is going to be one of my busy days, as tea is usually made with fresh spring water, and collecting the water from the well is one of my tasks; it is also one of my major challenges. The bucket definitely isn't child size and being made of tin feels heavy even when empty. The need is to get as much water as possible into the bucket and back home in order to avoid too many trips.

Sadly, this theory never really works since the handle is in proportion to the bucket size, but it is easy to work out if I can suspend the bucket from my arm, and hold it away from me, my movements shouldn't cause the water to slop over the side quite so much; holding it firmly, with both hands, at the base of the handle, and having to keep it at chest level guarantees that every step needs to be considered very carefully. The spring well is situated on the road side about fifty yards from the house. The road has lots of loose stones and leaving my shoes off cannot be a consideration this time. The art has to be in tipping the bucket slightly away from me, so that I don't become the target; with frequent rest stops it is possible to keep most of the water where it is needed. This is one occasion when being out-of-doors is far from ideal; sitting quietly and listening has its advantages too.

On this particular occasion, I didn't know that being sent to the spring is a deliberate attempt to get me out of the way for a short time, but what follows will be a guiding force throughout my life.

Over lunch there is much discussion about which trips to make, and on which days. The first trip is necessary for my grandmother's benefit; there must be a picnic at the seaside too, but that will depend on the weather. Eventually the conversation drifts to politics and the Emergency; all the rationing problems we are having, but no one really wishes to dwell on these issues for long and the Burren itself is a much more interesting topic to explore. My mother and aunt aren't local people, but are keen to know more about the area and its history, which pleases my grandfather, my grandmother, my father and my uncle because for them it means reminiscing.

'As the crow flies' is a comment which usually holds my attention; imagine being a crow and flying over things whilst being able to look down; oh, what fun and what a different way of seeing things. Later, when the Cliffs of Moher, which are visible from our house, are mentioned, my enthusiasm simply gets the better of me. '*Oh, how far is that as the crow flies?'* The presence of my aunt and uncle have given me confidence, but for a moment there is silence as a thought occurs to me - Oh dear now I am in trouble! But to my surprise there is a lot of laughter, which makes me feel uncertain, and I can see my mother and aunt exchange a glance and nod to each other. Shortly afterwards I am sent to get more water; oh, the indignity and uncertainty, and worse, arriving back with the water, I am sent out again to collect, of all things: bits of moss, odd shaped stones - especially some flat ones – pieces of shale, small flowers, and twigs. Oh, this is a different type of punishment and quite beyond my understanding. I set out with my bag thinking - They must all be living in a different fairy tale world to my imaginary one! On my return, however, I am so glad that my thoughts have remained just thoughts.

My aunt has often told me stories of the beautiful hats my mother used to make in Dublin; women would ask her, as a favour, to make a hat for a special occasion because "she had a magic touch". Yes, she makes clothes for my brothers and myself but there has been no evidence of the magic which my aunt spoke about; that is about to change and I will be able to see her creativity in action, but not in hat making. My trip to the spring provides an opportunity for the two ladies to discuss me in my absence. It is almost possible to guess the direction of the conversation; surely they would have been saying, *'She asks so many questions about this place and it is impossible to answer all of them. What can we do to keep her quiet?'*

Stored in boxes and tucked away in cupboards for many years, but now unpacked, is an amazing collection of materials: ribbons, feathers, buttons, beads and embroidery threads. They stand and wait as I enter and approach the table with my collection; their eyes fixed on my face, and they are not disappointed. I know that sometimes the thought of being given a fruity lollipop just makes my mouth water but now my eyes feel watery too. This has to be like Heaven: so many colours, like the colours of all the beautiful flowers and shrubs which I see regularly, and so many different textures; and all those beads and sequins. Oh my! And nobody says, 'You mustn't touch'; on the contrary I am told to 'put the fabric to my face and feel the texture'; doesn't it feel soft, or silky, or rough or smooth, and so on, and on…until I am dancing round in excitement, with fabric draped around me like a sari. The sheer joy of this moment is having the ladies join in the fun too; they are so happy and carried away. Just once I notice a very sad look on my mother's face, but then it is gone and she is laughing again, but reminding everyone that there is some serious work to be done. Initially the men ignore this distraction but the noise makes their private conversation impossible and they are soon caught up in the project. They all speak quietly for a few moments, and then they set to work, but why, oh why doesn't someone tell me! I was about to invent my own games with all these treasures but instead, I have to stand back to 'let the dog see the rabbit', as my father used to say when we got in the way. What an exercise in patience; it really is difficult this time but I watch and listen.

With so many teachers and an artist present, they have decided that it shouldn't be difficult to achieve their main aim, which is to give me a bird's eye view of the Burren area where we will be travelling later. What an afternoon; there is so much fun, laughter and argument as they try to achieve a likeness, with my mother directing the exercise. Out comes the grey fabrics, some silky and shiny, others are small pieces which are darker grey with very open weave, and then the blue fabric which has a water effect running through it and which glistens and changes, depending on where the light is and how one looks at it. Items have to be collected from the kitchen cupboard; a bread plate tucked under the shiny fabric creates a lovely plateau, and a small casserole needs to be used for the biggest mountain. Then there is a piece of dark grey lace – doubled – which is put over small objects, because uncle says that there are many very porous rocks there too. The blue fabric is needed to create the sea and, *'Now for your bag'*, they say. Oh, who could think about my bag, at a time like this; but I know there is still so much for me to learn. The moss becomes the cultivation and natural growth areas and, as moss is usually green on the top but gradually changes to brown at the base, it is easy to achieve the variety which they need. The multicoloured and multisized beads become the special touches where flowers appear; the small flowers and twigs substituted as trees.

'Where are the roads?' someone asks. Oh my, is there going to be an argument! Uncle is the chief navigator but he says, *'Nobody has asked about roads!'* This is great, I think we can hitch a ride on the back of the crow but perhaps now is not a good time to say so. There is a lot of head scratching, and then a new plan of action, which involves my grandfather, because he used to cycle on all these roads and knows all the landmarks and villages very well indeed. The mountains and the shrubbery need some adjusting, but soon it is time to lay the heavy greyish Aran wool down to provide the roads. Cork bottle tops of different sizes become the villages, and even Grandfather's pipe cleaners add a new dimension, representing some craggy areas. My stones become small boulders and the flat ones, which they had been so specific about, become the shale areas. Oh, and the cotton wool; yes, there was always lots of that around – it is good for bathing cuts and bruises. Now, however, it adds that final touch and becomes the waves round the coast.

After tidying all the edges, they all stand back and congratulate themselves on their achievements! But haven't they stopped to consider that little people have a different perspective to adults, and my view of the scene is limited to the outer edges! Then someone says it is time for me to see and I am lifted on to the edge of the table, where I stand looking down and get a glimpse of the vastness and diversity of this beautiful limestone region, 'as the crow flies'. They say that it is merely to give me an idea about geography and distance and places, but no one can create all that the crow sees. They can tell me how many miles it is from one village to the next, but not as the crow flies, at least not in the Burren and not yet. I try to make a lot of mental pictures because this beautiful creation will shortly need to be dismantled and the table used to prepare tea. There also needs to be final discussions about tomorrow's trip to Kilfenora with more and different questions. Oh, how lucky I am!

CHAPTER 8
SUMMER DRIVES TO KILFENORA

Yesterday we enjoyed our textile adventure; today in the kitchen it is warm and sunny and, as arranged, we plan to visit Ballybreen and Kilfenora after lunch. Grandma has taken so much care when getting ready, because this afternoon she wishes to look her best. She sometimes wears fitted blouses with a frilled collar and cuffs, and today is one of those occasions. The blouse has black and beige stripes which slant outwards from the centre, she calls it a chevron effect and, with black shiny buttons, it looks very special. Her skirt is A-shaped and made in darker beige than the stripe in the blouse; being full length the bottom is quite wide. Today she is wearing brown shoes with a strap and a little button, which has a tiny stud in the centre. She says to Mum, *'How do I look Annie?'* Mum replies, *'Wonderful, but aren't you going to wear your jet beads and earrings?'* Oh, now I'll be able to see them again, it's my favourite necklace made of jet, and she once let me touch it and it is as light as a feather. She has told me that the beads were made from ancient fossilised wood, and each bead was cut like a gem so that it reflects the light shining on it and doesn't seem to be just black anymore. When the light shines on all the beads the whole necklace sparkles and when I see her wearing it, and the earrings too, I think please, please, let me have those one day. Despite not being very well she looks happy today, but now we must wait until after lunch.

There is no time for excitement yet because my best clothes are still in the cupboard, and my grandma is waiting with the hair brush and ribbons. Having rushed about during the morning, my hair is now a tangled mess and there is only dreaded submission; so, head on lap and the strokes begin whilst trying not to hurt but managing to do so anyway. Oh dear, I mustn't stain her skirt with tears, but just hang on to them until later and maybe they will go away. Why, oh why can't I have hair like my brothers; they don't need this treatment. Eventually, happiness is restored, apart from those awful ribbons, which can't fall off accidentally; well, not for a while yet!

Shortly after lunch the waiting is over, and my aunt and uncle arrive, but because Mum is not coming with us, they stay for a cup of tea. This is my opportunity to have a good look at the new Ford car, but the old one had been a new vehicle to me, and how did this compare with our own transport? The main advantages are easy to see but so too are the disadvantages. The most important thing is that they all have wheels and this is my fascination – wheels and circles. How many times have I rolled myself into a tight ball, even then I can't achieve any speed no matter how long I practice when we are playing children's games; although it is always much better if we start at the top of the grassy hill, rolling to the bottom of the field near our house. I need to know so much about wheels; those on the cart have metal bands, the trap has rubber bands but these car wheels have so much rubber and the spokes are very different too. No more observations now, however, as the others have come to join me. Grandma sits in the front passenger seat because she wishes to chat with Uncle, and I will be in the back with Aunt, feeling very optimistic.

The road to Ballybreen, which is a mile outside Kilfenora, will only take about fifteen minutes. We drive past the Castle, which is our playground, and on through Lisdoonvarna, going south-east towards Kilfenora. This part of the route is not familiar to me, but it is very pleasant. There are lots of fields and a large pine forest. Now could be a good time for a stop, providing an opportunity to walk under the trees on the carpet of pine needles, but not without shoes! It looks lovely and cool in there, and with the sun shining through the trees, creates interesting shadows. There are undoubtedly some fascinating plants in there as well. Unfortunately the windows of this car are much closer to the roof than the last one, and it is difficult to see outside. Having my own seat, there isn't a need to sit on Aunt's knee, which would make it easier to see out, and bobbing up and down is strictly forbidden. It isn't a big problem, this time really, because I am also trying to listen to the conversation, and when the Burren is mentioned it seems a good time to say, '*Which day are we going to the Burren then?*'

Uncle has a very hearty laugh, and the sound of this now fills the car; looking at my aunt confirms my suspicion – they think it's funny. Oh, perhaps Grandma is taking me seriously - but oh no! She is smiling too. Looking at, but not through the side window helps me to remain composed until the laughter dies down and mercifully Uncle can explain.

'You know that beautiful table scene of the Burren, which your Mum inspired us to make yesterday?'

'Yes, I will have my mental pictures, forever.'

'*Good, and they are very important too, but there was so much we couldn't tell you then, because there was a lot happening and, even now, we can't tell you too much because you may not be able to take it all in. Also, we know that there is so much to be discovered about this place, as you call it, which means that we haven't got the whole picture either*'. Feeling much better now, it seems possible to ask a question!

'So, we are in the Burren now, please can you tell me a little more?'

It's Grandma who answers, '*That will have to wait for the return journey because we have now arrived at Ballybreen.*'

Within a few minutes we stop outside a large wrought-iron gate which is closed, and when Uncle gets out to open it, I overhear Grandma say, *'I'm not really looking forward to this and will feel better when the visit is over.'* We are visiting her brother's widow, but her heart is sad because this was once her home too. As a bachelor, her brother promised that my father would inherit this estate, but when he became confined to bed, he decided to marry his housekeeper. All this happened many years before I was born, and what had been a beautiful house – so the story goes – is now looking much neglected. The visit doesn't last very long, and soon we are heading back up the long driveway and Uncle has to stop and open the gate again. I can hear Grandma sigh.

After a very short drive we arrive at Kilfenora and Uncle parks the car. Grandma wishes to visit her brother's grave in the Cathedral graveyard, which is just the path width away from the main wall. Uncle helps her out of the car. There is a lovely old stone wall surrounding the Cathedral and the graveyard, but this is only the beginning!

As children we have been taught to have respect for the dead, who can no longer defend themselves. But, Lord it is so difficult to stay still because, although the graveyard is full of people who have died, and the Cathedral is ancient, crumbling in places, this place seems so alive. All the headstones are so different; there are some slabs, with domed tops in marble or stone, others with a cross on top, but there are so many very old ones as well, both short and tall, with a cross in a circle, and some with designs and symbols on. There is a marble inset in some of the taller ones, making it much easier to read the writing. Even here, however, the writing is fading on the very old stones. Many of the graves have surrounds, either stone or marble, and again the shapes vary. In the case of Great-uncle's grave, this is made of beige and white marble. The base of the cross, which includes the writing, is wide and deep, and supports a very tall cross in a circle. It is this which has me riveted. Why, why in a circle? I love drawing circles. That will be a good exercise in drawing; drawing circles is much easier than straight lines because it's continuous. A gentle tug at my aunt's sleeve and I whisper, *'Please can we look at the other graves?'*

'Alright, but we mustn't walk on them.' Oh, that's easy I can walk on the surrounds because my feet are small.

Leaving the others talking quietly, we walk around the graveyard looking more closely at inscriptions and designs, and soon arrive at the entrance to the Cathedral. The outside of the building isn't any grander than the Churches I go to, and it is so much smaller, but moving inside changes everything and size doesn't matter any more because, here too, there is a sense of 'aliveness' even though some of the roof is missing. It must be those ancient people speaking through their work, which is making it all feel alive. Aunt says that these are ancient sculptured monuments that I am looking at; there is so much to see but it is the window which dominates, and captivates. It has three large openings each recessed into its own space.

These openings are individually outlined in sculpture, which creates a strong frame, but at the same time seems to guide my gaze back to and through the openings.

Oh my, just imagine all those years ago standing here and watching the light and sun reflecting on these sculptures. These wonderful pieces were designed by man and sculpted in stone, which couldn't have been easy, but who and what had inspired them? There isn't time to gaze any longer now because there is something else my aunt wishes me to see before we go. I already feel as though I have been in this building for a long time!

Leaving the building, we move quickly to the end of the graveyard, where my aunt lifts me up so that I can look over the wall and get a glimpse of the enormous cross in the field beyond. Oh, oh, oh! '*That*', she says, '*is one of the most important high crosses in Ireland and, although you can't see from here, it has on the front the figure of Christ, with his arms outstretched; it is called a Celtic cross.*' I can only look, being quite incapable of more questions at this particular moment!

Grandma and Uncle have made their way back to the car, and we mustn't keep them waiting; but on our way through we stop to look at other broken pieces of pillars, which have beautiful engravings showing circles, patterns and figures on them. The patterns look just like the designs on the jumpers, which Mum knits for us. I can only point to these but my aunt understands and says, '*These are Celtic designs and you will see many, many more when you are older*'. When we return home some of the adults report to Mum that I have been very quiet on the way back. Well, whatever do they expect, just give me time to recover!

CHAPTER 9
KILFENORA, THE CATHEDRAL AND THE CELTS

Grandma declared this morning that, following yesterday's exertions, she would prefer to spend the afternoon in the garden. This is good news to my ears and I will quietly set about collecting extra water from the spring and offer Mum all the help she needs. Then I must be patient until Aunt and Uncle arrive, and I must decide which question is the most important: the Burren, Kilfenora or the Celts. The Burren is the area where we are living, and there will be other trips and opportunities to discuss it. The first priority must be the cathedral and then the celts. It was difficult last night not to dream about all those shapes and designs I had seen yesterday; I so want to know more about them and who created them, but I also hope to find out why the Cathedral is so small. There is really no need for me to worry, since Grandma is very proud of this place where she grew up, and as she used to say, *'It has its own cathedral you know!'*

Yesterday's visit has stirred her memories, and by the time we have drunk our first cup of tea in the garden she is eager to reminisce. Granddad and Uncle have heard it all before and seem happy to leave the ladies to have their own chat and I am eager to listen.

'The old home in Ballybreen was a lovely place set amongst the trees, but Kilfenora, our village, was within a short walking distance. It is a small inland village, approximately eight and a half miles from Ballinalacken, where we are now. It's about the same distance from Lahinch where, as you know, there is a beautiful beach, and about twelve miles to the north is Ballyvaughan. Our village is laid out in such a way that it has a large market place close to the Cathedral. The farmers bring their cattle and produce from miles around on market day; the surrounding lands are so rich and productive. As well as the shop and the post office, there are two public houses, but the main attraction is the cathedral and the Celtic crosses found there. It didn't really become a

Cathedral until 1152, when there was a meeting at Kells to decide where the centre of the diocese would be. The meeting was called the Synod of Kells, and before this Kilfenora Church was a monastery. It was Saint Fachtnan who founded the Monastery in the 6th Century and built the original church there, which will have been made of wood. What was happening in those days was that saints such as St Fachtnan lived often alone but more usually with other monks in small communities, perhaps no more than half a dozen people. They were very religious, living frugally in huts, devoting their lives to prayer and worship, with manual labour at the centre of things. As time passed others joined them and from these very humble beginnings quite large monasteries developed. When it became the Episcopal see, Kilfenora was the smallest diocese in Ireland.

In 1055 Murchad O'Brien had burned down a stone church there, which over the years had replaced the earlier wooden one, but another was built sometime between 1056 and 1058. This building didn't last long either as it too was burned in 1100, but this time by accident; our present cathedral was restored some time later.

Kilfenora was also known as the City of Crosses, and its new status was commemorated on one of them. There were supposed to have been seven crosses at one time but not all remain, one of the main crosses stands in the field to the west of the Cathedral.' Oh, that had to be the cross I saw yesterday when Aunt lifted me onto the wall. Well, now is definitely not the time to interrupt. And Grandma continues, *'For many years the Cathedral was used by Catholics and Protestants for their services, but in 1840 St. Fachtna's Roman Catholic Church was built not very far from the there, and this was our family Church; but Kilfenora didn't really have the population to support both financially, especially after the famine in 1845. And anyway many people were without a proper income, and there was a lot of hardship. But now I think that it really is time for another cup of tea'.*

We could see that emotionally this has been a tiring journey and, leaving her chatting with my aunt, Mum and I go inside to prepare tea and scones. Granddad and Uncle can't have been very far away, because as soon as they hear the hustle and bustle in the kitchen they reappear. Oh, wouldn't it be wonderful if one of them could talk some more about the Cathedral and the people who had made the Crosses. Not wishing to be tiresome and eager to help, I carry the scones through to the garden. The adults continue to chat about local history, but for a short while the scones need all my attention.

With tea over, and all my efforts very much appreciated, everyone knows that I am impatient to know more. It is Uncle who looks at me and says, using his favourite expression, *'Well Young Lady, what would you like to know now; your Grandma is dozing and we will be here until she wakes up?'* That puts me on the spot and now I have to think really hard again! I hadn't expected such a direct question, and he sounds a bit like my schoolteacher. I do have a lot of questions and I know they will have many of the answers, except Mum who came from County Mayo and Aunt who comes from County Meath, and they will have questions of their own. So I'll ask about the Celts in Ireland and wait and see what happens. But now, having asked, I know that he is finding it difficult because he is taking a long time to begin.

'Well, the story of the people who came to Ireland many years ago is a long and complicated one, and it could be very difficult to make it short and easy for you to understand, but living in the Burren, and not in Dublin where your aunt and I live, means that you may find it easier to use your imagination.

I grew up here too you know, and have a feeling for the Celtic race or The Celts as they are called. The people of Ireland have changed and developed in so many ways since that time, and I have no doubt the change will continue in the future. Much has yet to be discovered about the Celts, as we know so little at present, but one thing we do know is that they have left us a lasting and enduring legacy. It isn't merely the geology of the Burren which fascinates us, it is the starkness of the landscape that they survived in, and not only survived but thrived here too.'

Looking towards the others he said *'I think this time we will allow the young lady to call the shots',* whatever that meant, and he turned to me and said, *'Would you like to ask the questions and we will try to answer as best we can!'*

'Oh, yes, I just want to know what made them tick, where did they get their ideas from, and did they have schools and universities?'

'Well! Firstly, tick is not an appropriate word to use; did you hear it at school? Secondly, you must think carefully and start at the beginning'. Goodness, this is worse than being in the classroom. Feeling a bit deflated I ask if it might be possible to use my own special list: who am I, where did I come from, how do I live, how do I learn, and maybe I will add some more. Everyone is nodding in agreement, except Grandma, who is nodding off.

CHAPTER 10
WHO WERE THE CELTS

So, as my Dad always says, first things first. 'Who were the Celts?'

Uncle says, *'If you were to look in the dictionary you will find a definition for the Celts which says: A member of a race of Central and Western Europe, described by the Romans as tall, blond, and large-bodied; or an individual of any of the various Celtic-speaking peoples, including the ancient Gauls and Britons and the modern Bretons, Welsh, Irish, and Gaelic Scotch. This also includes the Isle of Man, where the language is called Manx, spoken only on the Isle of Man, where your Dad and Mum spent their honeymoon, but maybe you can ask them about that, and you may even go there one day. But all these spoken languages are slightly different, because they have developed independently in their own regions and over a long period of time.*

If we are thinking about who these people were, we would have to look back almost to the beginnings of civilization, because they are a small part of the whole of mankind; like a little cog in the big world wheel. Civilization began towards the end of the Ice Age, after that came the Stone Age; this was followed by the Bronze Age, which developed around 2,000 BC. Those letters BC may be unfamiliar to you, but you will come across lots of dates later having the suffix BC, which means Before Christ, and AD, which signifies Anno Domini and is Latin for the year of the Lord.' Goodness me, there's a question for later. Why couldn't they stick with English, or Latin, which I haven't even started to learn yet? How will I ever understand?

'As I said, the Bronze Age started about 2000 BC, and it continued until 700 BC when the Iron Age emerged. It was at this time that the Celts existed and they were referred to as the Men of Iron. You will be happy to know that each age period is recognized by the tools which were used during that time,

and also how those implements were utilised. From the very beginning man only had stone, but from this he created the means whereby he could survive and develop too.

Stone Age man needed to do what your Dad is always telling you to do – keep your wits about you and use your imagination – because each person is given very special gifts when he is created, but he must learn how to use them, and always listen carefully to his inner voice whilst being aware of what is happening about him. 'Necessity is the mother of invention' happens to be my favourite expression, because I believe this to be motto which was put to good use by all those ancient people. I have so much admiration for them, because they started with nothing and learned through the dent of their own perseverance, while using the gifts they were born with. They learned to think for themselves. Of course, thinking – even thinking up stories – takes a lot of discipline and can be hard work, and I believe this would be a very good time to say, Annie, wouldn't a cup of tea go down well?'

And didn't we all need a drink! Thank heavens for all the water collected this morning; going to the well now would be unthinkable, and Grandma would surely come round in my absence. Somehow though I now feel that collecting the water will never again seem such a chore; I have a bucket to carry the water and shoes to protect my feet, but those ancient people didn't have anything except their gifts, imagination and determination.

It is good to stop and think about what Uncle has told us because, although he is telling it as a story, he is talking about real people who had been born; had lived and died leaving us so much to see, talk about and learn from.

I can see that the adults are enjoying their tea while I have fizzy orangeade, which is a rare treat but, oh my, how the fizziness tickles the back of my throat and nose, which makes me want to sneeze. No time for that now though, as I need to think about the next question - where did I come from, that's a big question! Now where is Granddad?

Throughout Uncle's story Granddad has been sitting with his eyes closed and looking as though he might soon be nodding with Grandma; he is growing old too, but unlike Grandma he isn't ill. Each time there has been a silence though, he has opened his eyes wide, looking straight at Uncle Ben, and as we stop for tea he vanishes into his bedroom. I don't understand because he never has a lie down in the middle of the afternoon, and anyway he would have said so, but why is he gone so long? His tea is almost cold by the time he returns, but he is looking so pleased with himself and doesn't seem to be aware of this because clasped in his hand are some apparently long forgotten maps. They are not very large, probably the size of my notebook which I use to practice my writing. We all realise now that he wants to tell his part of the story. He tells us that his interest in travelling first started when, as a boy, he listened to the readings from the Bible, and became fascinated with the place names. He had made some drawings from his Atlas and filled in all those places mentioned, hoping one day to visit some of them.

Looking at Mum, who is busily knitting an Aran sweater for one of the family, and more concerned about keeping her children warm in the winter than in the history of far-off places, he says, *'Of course Annie, this journey is not merely about those people who travelled from one country to another, as we hear about in the Bible, it is also the story of how the Celts and their language, and even your knitting pattern has travelled from Europe to reach us here, adapting and changing slightly on the different journeys'*. Oh, that has got to her; she drops a stitch while looking at Granddad and laughing, because they both know she hasn't been paying very much attention. Of course she has been thinking about looking after her visitors too, and preparing a meal for later. Grandma isn't listening either, and she will be very upset when she knows because she loves travelling. Now, however, everything is put aside as Granddad continues.

'Well, as your Uncle Ben said earlier, we believe the Celts emerged in Europe about 700 BC. They were nomads who had a restless spirit and travelled from region to region, but some

would remain and become more established, absorbing whatever culture already existed, and also creating more of their own. They had not only discovered iron but had perfected the right temperature to enable them to mould it as they wished, and their tools and weapons were more sophisticated and efficient than those of the earlier inhabitants. This gave them a great deal of power, but according to the tales we hear, they didn't always use it wisely. Although they are supposed to have started in Eastern Europe, over a period of two hundred years they had migrated to countries known as Asia Minor, Greece, Italy, Spain, and France. We can look at these places now on the maps and see how they travelled, by land and sea, taking their knowledge with them.

They arrived in Britain and Ireland about 500 BC. Now here we can use our imagination! We know that sea trade was well established at that time, and it is easy to visualise groups arriving in Ireland in the same way that many Irish people left during the Famine period and at other times. There wouldn't have been a mass invasion and there wasn't a mass exodus but a steady flow. The Celts weren't at war with either country, they were merely following their nomadic instincts.'

Well, I could understand that story too. Grandma had been opening and closing her eyes for the last few minutes, but she is now wide awake and, with a cup of tea to revive her, is soon very spritely and keen to know what has been happening. Everyone contributes a little and then she looks at me, hoping that I have been listening, and will be ready to add my piece which, of course, I will but what follows is another question. Well I now know about who they were and where they came from, but I need to know how did they live, and learn, and feel inside because I am trying to understand.

So Grandma adds her contribution, *'I am not really sure where to start, but I know that there are some things you may remember from school.'* My smile seemed to be the only answer she needs, and soon she is being a school-mam again. Oh, but this is going to be interesting, provided she doesn't question me afterwards and expect me to remember everything.

I know she is very good at heart, even though she may be out of sorts at times when she can be a bit of a madam really. All the same I had better create a picture in my mind and be prepared.

One superior look and everyone is paying attention as she goes on:

'Everything we see around us has a creative story, but the first creation story is the greatest and the most popular, because it is about the creation of the universe and the world in which we live. Now, if your Mum was going to make a cake she would need to collect together all the ingredients and then go through the various stages, bringing them all together in the right order, which is most important if she wants something to bake or make something nice, which we can all enjoy.

The creation of the universe is similar, in that it needed to have a sense of order; the heavens and the earth; dark and light, night and day; water, land and sky. Then there were the extra lights to divide night from day and create an order for the seasons; these were called the sun, moon and stars. The next stage, once there was land and water, was filling the land with grass, plants and trees of all types, which produced seeds, which would multiply. Following this the water was filled with living, moving creatures, big and small and which continued to grow in number; so too, with the sky which was filled with living creatures called fowl, birds and insects, created with wings so that they could fly. The land produced a whole range of different living creatures and livestock, including wild animals and, of course, all the creepy crawlies which you don't like much.

Finally, man appeared, but he would not have lived as we do for a very long time; he would have had to learn 'how to survive'. He couldn't live as the birds do because he hadn't got wings; he couldn't live like the water creatures do, because he hadn't been created for this, and he wouldn't have wanted to crawl for that same reason. He was, in fact, more like the animals, and would have lived like them at first, eating berries and plants: hunting wild animals or fishing in the rivers and the lakes. He would also have noticed how animals bonded, forming groups or herding, where the eldest cared for and were protective of their young. It was rather like small communities in areas which they will have fought for or established for themselves. Fighting only occurred when other animals, or even one of their own breed, tried to move in and take over. Younger, dominant, competitive members would eventually leave the group or be driven out, and move on to new territory where they would start afresh.

Over a period of hundreds of thousands of years man developed, and learned to live a separate type of existence where he became more civilized. For you, my dear, civilized means being refined in taste and manner but we will talk about that another time'.

Oh, that was a beautiful story. She hasn't said much about how they would have been feeling but then she couldn't know that, and perhaps it came through in the caring and protective part. I can't possibly ask any more questions now, because this has taken its toll on everyone and I need time to think carefully about all that has been said. But I must remember to say thank you, as I collect the numerous cups and saucers, because I know that they have done it all for my benefit. What a pity my brothers weren't here too, but never mind because on one of our long winter evenings I will tell them myself.

CHAPTER 11
ORIGINS OF THE CELTS

Following on that exciting story this afternoon, I wondered what might happen this evening because the subject had continued to dominate their conversation. Well, Grandma has retired early but because we are on holiday and have visitors, there is no pressure on the children to go to bed, and so we are seated in the kitchen – this is usually the perfect time and place for story telling, but mainly for the elders; we are normally sent off to bed and told to behave. On occasions this command simply encourages us to rebel; if we haven't used up all our energy, pillows so carefully made by Mum, using ticking and duck feathers, become the perfect weapons for knocking human targets off the throne. Feathers, especially duck down which are the softest, are really difficult to collect and Mum has learned that the only compromise is to reinforce the seams. This, however, is not going to happen this evening, because everyone is relaxed with their favourite 'toddy' – mine has to be milk, but the boys don't waste their time indoors on bright summer evenings and have gone to do their own thing.

I was very conscious this afternoon of one person who was missing, but who would have been happy to have been involved. As Dad has completed his chores for the day, he is with us now and, like Grandma, when she has been napping, wishes to know what we have been doing. Once again there is a resumé – that's what they call it – then Dad looks at me with a twinkle in his eye, which challenges me to come up with another question. They know me very well indeed and there is one on the tip of my tongue, but first it is necessary to examine my checklist. Now this is a problem for me because there are too many questions and I can't decide which should really come next.

Last time Uncle had said that I should 'call the shots', so now I have to fire a number off and tell them I need their help in finding the right order, and I must do it quickly because I don't know when we will all be together again, and it seems such a big topic. OK, Uncle had said it would be difficult and now I know, so here goes!

'Why did the Celts come to Ireland? Were there any people here already? If there were people here, did they fit in with them? Would they have travelled the same route as Granddad said? Did any leave and go back to where they came from? Well, Uncle keeps coming back to visit and Dad is back here to live, but I know how that came about.'

When I stop for breath there is a burst of laughter and Uncle says, looking at Dad, '*Where did you find her?*' That seems a bit disrespectful but before I can become agitated he says, *'Your Dad is very good at history and I think we will all be glad to listen to what he has to say.'*

Dad is scratching behind his ear as he is thinking and then says, *'You may have to accept one long answer which will cover as many questions as possible.'*

Oh, and I have just remembered a most important one, but I can't interrupt now.

I am not quite sure what is in his glass, but it has come from a crystal glass container, which has a stopper in it and, of course, no label to tell me what it is. These containers are untouchable where we children are concerned. Whatever it is it has a really horrible smell; nobody minded one day when I gently removed the stopper, just to reassure myself, because nobody saw me. The smell doesn't seem to worry him though, and before he starts he upends the glass and drinks the contents. I suppose there wasn't much in the glass but we children have been told not to gulp. Extending it to Mum for a refill, he begins.

'*From what I have been hearing it seems that you have covered the Who, Where, and How aspect of the story, and we will continue with the others, but first I believe it might help if you quickly find your pencil and pad'*. Oh, why! The others didn't need anything like that and, heavens, where have I put them. As I move around, pretending to know, his voice follows me. '*Since you have a fascination for circles and wheels, I think it might help you now to draw a wheel with a purpose, or better still, let me do this one for you.'* At last success, and as I reseat myself near the corner of the table, where my glass is resting, he takes the pad and draws a circle which fills the page, and then in the centre he puts a heavy dot explaining that this would be the Celts. He then draws six evenly spaced lines outwards and adds: -

1. WHO were they?
2. WHERE did they come from?
3. HOW did they live/learn?
4. WHY did they come to Ireland?
5. WHICH route did they take?
6. WHAT is their legacy?

That looked really good, especially as it included the most important question, number six, because that is why we started on this story in the first place, and hopefully at the end I will have a rounded picture. As he is finishing off the drawing I am busy ruminating – this is one of Granddad's favourite words, but when I asked him one day what it meant, he said it was like chewing the cud, which made me giggle as I told him I had often watched the cows doing that – it seemed to be their special thing – but I reminded him that I didn't do that! He said he knew, but ruminating was exactly like that, meditating or going back over the same idea. Whatever, I had better stop it now because we are ready to go forward again, but backwards in time and, heavens, we are going round in circles too.

One more sip from his glass and we can all see that, although he is talking to me, his mind is far away.

'The reason for the circle, which seems to dominate drawings you often make, is that so many things work in that way. Life is like that, we arrive as helpless beings and end our lives as helpless beings too; it's really the circle of our existence on earth, but the spirit which we are born with, and which is our being, lives on afterwards. The seasons of the year move in the same way, there is no beginning or end but continuous movement. The Universe itself controls the order of things and we have no say in how it operates, we simply accept

that it is, and each individual is simply a minute part of that giant wheel. Because I sometimes see you examine the wheels of the cart very carefully, knowing as I do that one of the spokes is damaged and will need to be replaced soon, I believe you understand that in order to keep the wheel turning safely, particularly when the load is heavy, there has to be change when things wear out. The Universe orders all change, including the tides, which you will be aware of when you stand outside and look down towards the sea, especially when it's as calm as a mill pond, but also the change seen when it's a raging force in nature, carrying all things before it. We can do nothing to stop it but we can enhance it and move with it, as is easily seen when sailing ships travel across the oceans. Without changing the essential forces we need to know how it has come about, since our beliefs are the essence of our being and without them life and change would be pointless.

The essence of our belief is what we call our spirit, and it is this spirit of life which gives everything its true meaning. One day you may draw another circle and in the centre put spirit, then make your own spokes, remembering that the real strength lies in the centre of the wheel, which sends out energy along the spokes to the outer edge. For instance when we are travelling in the cart and go over a rut or large stone the outer band takes the impact, but it also jars the spokes which lead back to the centre. Since we are all like individual wheels, it follows that whatever is happening about us will affect us in some way or another. I tell you this now because we are discussing those people who seem to have captured your imagination; I can't explain one without also looking at the other, it is by way of giving you a centre for your own wheel. But right now the centre of our wheel is the Celts.

I know the whole of this story already because your Granddad and Grandma told your uncles and me when we were young. That is why we feel you should know, then you in turn can pass it on. You see, it is by word of mouth that the story of the Celts has survived. They didn't have a written language and some scholars become frustrated because there is no written proof to read, digest, change or distort. Even if they had been able to write they probably wouldn't have seen a need to record their experience. The Celts were a living, breathing, working people dedicated to surviving by relying on their closeness, companionship, dependency and community spirit, but most of all they relied upon the truth of their spoken word as they saw it. Anything else would have been pointless.

To understand all this more fully we can consider briefly again the first three spokes, and how it all began, because they themselves were the legacy of what had gone before.

They discovered iron, which distinguished them from their predecessors. Farming had already been established before the existence of the Celts, and they became wealthy and powerful by its exploitation, but as they are remembered as men of iron it was the discovery and the uses of this metal which set them apart. The Celts and their forebears survived because they had incredible observation, imagination, determination and intuition. Unfortunately there was one other thing which they all had in common – a total lack of understanding about the source of and reason for creation itself. They venerated the earth, with its abundant provision, as Mother Earth; they could see how everything grew and developed; they recognised that they were part of this process and that their being did not come to an end when they died. They could experience the elements (earth, water, wind and fire) or at least the effects of these. They observed the movement of the sun and the moon, and the changing tides, as well as seasons and weather patterns which caused so much chaos in the sky, affecting all they did and tried to achieve. For instance, our progress on the farm is very dependant on what is happening in the sky, and we hope and pray for the right weather conditions to allow us to save our crops. Our knowledge has given us a more rounded understanding of the nature of the whole system, and this in years to come will be developed much further.

For our ancient ancestors though, and by that I mean as far back as we are aware, this knowledge wasn't available, and whilst they worshipped nature's provision, which they could see, they didn't understand how or why it was so. They believed there must be many powerful beings above, which caused this to happen and because they didn't understand, they were afraid of this power and what it could do to them, and everything around them. You know already that the term God refers to a supernatural omnipotent being, who is worshipped as having power over nature and human fortunes. They, and their predecessors, could only attribute this title to those things they could see, such as the sun, the moon, wind, rain, fire, thunder, animals, trees and other things, and they invented individual gods as a means of obtaining the power to control them. They hoped to achieve this by making sacrifices and performing rituals for whichever god they needed a favour from. If their wishes and needs weren't met they believed that the particular god they had appealed to was angry with them. They would then make greater sacrifices – including human ones – in their attempt to succeed. Although it is believed that the lengthy rituals involved much symbolism, we know that some of the stories we have heard are just myths, and the writers have used their imagination to paint a more interesting picture.

There are two words that I should give you before we go any further; they may help you but they are not to provoke extra questions right now!' Oh, Heaven forbid. I can't think now! It's taking me all my time to keep up and I have to concentrate! '*You can look them up in the dictionary another time as they have a number of meanings. The first word is myth, for instance a story where the origin is forgotten, which is part of history but helps to explain some practice or belief. The other word you need is Druid, because this is the word most commonly associated with the Celts and their beliefs. We know, however, that their early beliefs were pagan, which means the worship of many gods rather than the one true God, as we do, and it started long before Christianity came into being.*

Many of the rituals, which they practiced, are still with us today in the things we see and do. Even in Church you will see that we have symbols, rituals and mysteries, which have changed, so that we worship the one God who is Creator of all. As the year progresses, you will come across festivals, which are a legacy from those earlier times; Harvest Thanksgiving and Halloween, for instance.

As I said earlier none of this was recorded on paper and yet the legacy or story can be seen all about us, in the circles, and the mounds which we call fairy mounds. The most important record though is engraved on stone, particularly the high crosses that have so many designs and symbols on them. This could, in a way, remind us of the Stone Age people, who had to find the best means of surviving; similarly for the Celts there was a spiritual need to discover something which might stand the test of time. Isn't it the Crosses at Kilfenora Cathedral which have fired your imagination and given us all such an exciting headache?

It would take the coming of Christianity in the third or fourth centuries that would effect the change necessary to overcome the pagan traditions, which were so brutally archaic. Christianity in Ireland pre-dates the coming of St. Patrick, by how many years we don't know, but it was the patron saint of our land who primarily won over the kings and the people to the true faith. This is not to say that the heritage of our Celtic ancestors was completely usurped by the new faith. In fact, as I have already said, many pagan traditions were assimilated into the practices of the new church, and in this way the people were more easily won over. A good example of this is the rededication of pagan holy sites to the worship of the God of Christianity.'

My goodness, we have almost come round in another circle, but he has made it easier for me to understand. What everyone here needs now is a good strong cup of tea and some of Mum's fruit cake. That was the order and I was eager to help, even though mine would be more milk. Throughout the tea break they all continue to discuss the topic; it seems that this is an opportunity for them to look at these fascinating issues and explore new ideas and thoughts in the light of more recent discoveries. But they are talking faster and using words which have no meaning for me.

Believing that they won't miss me for at least ten minutes I am going outside to stand, once more, and look down towards the sea.

The sun is setting now, casting a beautiful warm red glow over the calm blue water, and picking out the little waves which glisten as they change from white to pink and ripple onwards towards the shore. How I would love to be down there watching the waves more closely as they gently roll over my feet. It is easy, however, to think back to other days when it looked as though the force behind the waves would drive them up the hill with a mighty roar. What an awesome thought! But if I don't get back before I'm missed there may be uproar inside too. After all, I have got them going and now need and want to go with them.

They have, in fact, just noticed my absence because they have been discussing who should be the next storyteller and the lot seems to have fallen back to Uncle. Oops! Now I am going to be a young lady again but where will he take me this time.

'There has always been argument and discussion concerning the history and geography of the world and that includes Ireland. Writers will go on developing theories which will be based on discovery, and this is our attempt to create a picture we hope you will understand.

In order to look at the route the Celts may have travelled, you need to go back in time once more but focus on Ireland, because they were not the first inhabitants of this land. It is said that the first people to inhabit Ireland arrived about 6000 BC, having crossed the narrow channel between Scotland and Ulster. They spread along the north and east coast and would have discovered the upper river Bann, which rises in the Mourne Mountains, County Down, and flows into Lough Neagh near Charlestown, County Armagh. They would have used this waterway to explore the island more deeply. In your absence we have been discussing other possibilities, and also the best means of explaining those ideas to you. Your Dad said it should be simple because of an experience you had last winter.' I look at Dad for reassurance, hoping that he hasn't been telling tales, and his smile means it is OK. *'He has told us that you like to fill your glass squash bottles with spring water from time to time, filling them to the brim and screwing the cap on tightly. Last winter a few of those you stored outside were covered with snow and then froze. When the snow thawed, and you wanted to retrieve the bottles, they had shattered. As he probably explained to you then, this was not the effect of the snow and ice around the bottles, but due to the expansion of the water as it froze. In the same way you can imagine that the effect of the Ice Age on the seawater, which moved as it froze, caused the sea levels to drop.*

We know that about 18,000 years ago Britain and Ireland were joined to Europe and that large parts of the seabed were exposed. Eventually though, the big freeze which caused this to happen came to an end; then very slowly the thaw began, which would again affect the land and sea level, and not all would have been as it was before the Ice Age. No one can really be sure about exactly how long this took, but as the ice melted the sea levels began to rise and flood the land. Or maybe, to put it another way, the melting ice flowed towards the sea, but some low lying land areas remained flooded.

Whatever the natural order, there were areas where the different countries were still joined, and if you look at your maps later you will see that parts of Scotland remain close to Ulster. Whilst the thaw continued, and the levelling of water was taking place, there would remain for a long time strips of land which connected us to our neighbours. For instance, you will see that, as well as Scotland and Ulster, there are places called Anglesey and Fishguard in Wales, which remain close to Dublin and Wexford, and because of this we believe that they were the last areas to be submerged. This would have allowed movement of animals and humans between Britain and Ireland over a considerable period of time.

In fact, there are one or two further theories we could examine now. Thomas, have you got your large map stored with the little ones you showed us earlier? We could have a look at both now'. Granddad nodded and disappeared to find them. He didn't hurry these days and I thought this would be an opportunity for me to collect my own thoughts together, but it wasn't to be and Uncle simply carried on.

'I know this story is a bit like your clock on the wall over there - the pendulum moves back and forth – but, in order to help you understand better, we need to look back at the order of development and progress. So, imagine those very early people needing to provide for themselves and their families; their basic needs were food, clothing and shelter. One source of food would also provide the beginnings of a revolution in man's approach to survival and progress. I know you don't like to talk about the pig, but it is a very useful and real example for now. When it is slaughtered here each year, full use is made of all the useable organs. Even the unusable pieces are buried in the ground and decay, eventually providing nourishment for the soil. We have no use for the bones except to boil them and give them to the dogs. The pig though, is one animal which is not usually skinned, but there are many which are and our ancestors quickly discovered this. They learned to treat the hides, which were saved and used to protect their own bodies from the elements. But a little bird has told us the story of the lamb in the storm.' Ooh, I wish they wouldn't talk about me in my absence. *'It was a lovely story and showed us that you care, but you learned that caring can sometimes be a problem, and that is something that you can add to your own wheel which your Dad has spoken about. You know now that the lamb has oil in its coat, which makes it waterproof. The skin also has oil in it, which improves as the animal grows and develops fat underneath. With proper preparation these skins had many uses. For instance, they were used for covering the early huts which provided shelter; for protecting the underside of the first small boats, when pieced together they made excellent tents, and you have seen the leather handbags which your Mum and Aunt use. The strips used to join the pieces are called thonging, and are also made*

from the animal skins. They had another particular use but we will come back to that later.

At this point Granddad comes in, hands the large map to Uncle who invites everyone to join him around the kitchen table. I am allowed to kneel on the high stool in order to get a better view. When we are all settled he takes up his story again.

'To continue with our theories then, and looking at the map of England and Ireland, the land bridges, which I mentioned earlier, would have allowed a number of huge still water lakes to develop before the banks were engulfed by natural and sea water, giving us what we now call the Irish sea.

The main reason for exploring this theory is to look at when and how sea travel began, whilst stretching our own thinking at the same time. So, the ancients would have observed the various items which floated on water, such as leaves, branches and even trees. They were not short of courage and imagination, and would quickly have discovered a means of stringing logs together, and finding a way of propelling them. This is probably the earliest and most primitive form of water transport, but they would have progressed to using hollowed out tree trunks, and later developed craft, using skins around a framework and animal fat to provide the waterproofing.

This method of transport would have been tested initially on calm waters, such as rivers or lakes, eventually being used on the Mediterranean sea and proving very useful as the most effective form of travel around the various seas and ports. The Atlantic Ocean would have presented a different problem, but one they would have resolved over time, and this would have allowed them to travel and explore wider regions. The main reason for the detour around this story is that we believe that what is now the Irish sea was, for a considerable period of time, a series of lakes, and there is little doubt that man could have reached the east coast of Ireland anywhere from Larne in Ulster down to Rosslare in Wexford. If we identify where the

Isle of Man is situated, we can see that it provides an ideal break in the journey at the wider points. Here, however, we are talking about the arrival of the first inhabitants about 6000 years BC, who would have come through Scotland, England and Wales, having migrated originally from Europe.

Using the same line of reasoning here and looking at the map, we can see that the shortest distance between Europe and England at present is between Calais and Dover. What is interesting too is that some of these original crossings are more or less the same sea routes in use today.'

They have all been leaning forward while peering at the map as they listened, but now stand upright with various exclamations as they rub their backs. The ladies declare a need for another hot drink but the men say they need something stronger, but no more for me at this time. What a pity! I'm sure squash would help to sort my thoughts out, whereas the milk seems to be making me drowsy, but there is just one more question I need to ask. Organising the drinks hasn't changed the topic of discussion which has become general. When we are all seated again Mum notices my fidgeting and realises that it is way past my bedtime, and tells Uncle that any more questions will need short answers.

'*OK,*' says Uncle, *'there is time then for one quick one before bed.'*

'Yes, I am wondering if they made different shaped huts, making them waterproof, did that help them to understand how to make boats?'

'Oh, I can see that you have been looking at pictures of very early boats, earlier than the currachs out in Doolin which the fishermen use. Don't forget those currachs are also used by the locals to travel between here and the Aran Islands too. But yes, you are probably right because this was all about learning, and they were very wise in so many ways. But now I can see you look tired and we will be here again tomorrow, besides there isn't much more to this part of the story, and we need time to think and talk before we can go any further.'

Dad has slipped away to find the boys but I thank them and beat a hasty retreat. Tonight I am happy to dream about explorers and boat building.

CHAPTER 12
CREATIVITY AND THE CELTS

After a good night's sleep my head is fully restored and I am eagerly looking forward to Aunt and Uncle's visit this afternoon. It is a lovely, warm, sunny day and Grandma, having had a quiet day yesterday, wants to get away from the house and visit Doolin, where she will sit in the car and enjoy the sea, or use the rug and sit with us outside. Grandma asks Mum, '*Will you come with us and have a rest too!*' I am delighted when she says, '*Yes, I think I will.*' It will of course mean that I will need to sit on someone's knee in the back of the car, but this is good news as I can see more as we drive along. The view won't really distract me though, because there is the story to complete. Mum has actually whispered on the way out to the car, that I mustn't make a nuisance of myself, but they all know that I can't wait.

Our destination is only about five miles away, but the roads are narrow and windy and Uncle drives slowly; hopefully there will be enough time to complete the story. It is Aunt Alice who opens the door to this wonderland. She asks '*Have you enjoyed all you have heard so far?*'

'*Oh yes, I have lovely pictures of people doing so many creative things with their hands, wondering, whilst doing so, how they could make things better.*' Granddad is always saying that many hands make light work, and two heads are better than one. He has also said that it is good to think alone, especially if there are major problems, but his favourite saying when under pressure is, Thought is a man in his wholeness, wholly attending, and I need time to think. He had been thinking too, because over breakfast he told me that, when he woke up this morning, he was considering what I needed to know next and how important it was not to complicate the stories. I thought he was about to launch into it himself but sadly he said he would explain to our visitors, when they arrived, and allow them to continue the story. Well, I must be content with that but I do love to listen to him! Of course Aunt Alice also recognises my needs and she continues.

'Yes, my Dear, that was how they progressed: by thinking, by using their imagination, and sharing their thoughts or, as we might say, throwing all ideas into one hat. So, now that you understand how people travelled, we can do a leap from those early days around 6000 BC to 2000 or 1800 BC; knowing that large seaworthy ships had been developed, which were capable of ocean crossings. You will understand too, when you look at the Atlantic rollers from outside your home, just how strong the ships needed to be, and sadly there were times when they weren't strong enough to cope with the waves, and ships and their passengers were lost. But we do know that by the year 1800 BC ships were trading between Ireland and Europe, and by that I mean that ships were bringing goods and commodities to, and taking goods from Ireland, and it is this trade which we are interested in.

Although it is still well before the arrival of the Celts, we can create another image here as a background. We have said that the Irish were already flourishing; they would have continued to develop the skills which they used when they first arrived and, as sea trade developed in new commodities, they would have extended their knowledge and developed further skills, producing for themselves replicas of items which they had acquired from the people who travelled on the ships, some of whom would undoubtedly have stayed. Many ancient items discovered here help us to be aware of those things which they possessed and used. For instance, we know that the first metalworkers had reached Ireland by 1800 BC, and were exploiting copper deposits in many parts. By the way, one of the reasons your Granddad discussed this with us earlier is that, as you already know, he was born in Cork, and Cork and Kerry are known to be two of the main copper mining areas, with Mizen Head in Cork being the more productive of the two. Have a look at your map later and you will see that Mizen Head is Ireland's most south-westerly point, but the rugged beauty of the whole of that area would make it difficult for shipping, and it is likely that sea travellers would have used Cobh or Bantry Bay as their ports just as we do today.

Although copper became, for a time, one of their main exports, they used it themselves too in order to produce bronze. You probably haven't come across this yet, but bronze is a mixture of copper and tin. The tin would have had to be imported from Cornwall and Spain. Other exports included daggers and axes and a type of spear with a bronze head called a halbert; these would have been exported to Europe. Although there is no evidence of any gold mines in Ireland, we know that gold ornaments were made and also exported at a later date. Oh, here we are in Doolin and we'll finish this shortly but let's get ourselves sorted first.

One of the reasons for coming to Doolin is to visit the tearooms, and Grandma will have an opportunity to chat with the lovely lady, with snowy white hair, who owns the shop. Her name is Miss Murphy, and people who come from far and wide receive a very warm welcome and enjoy her delicious homemade scones and tea. Doolin is little more than a fishing village, but with tremendous appeal. It seems to have been carved out of the countryside by the forces of nature, creating a rugged rock strewn cove, which we believe was used once upon a time by smugglers and the like. Within a few miles of Doolin are the spectacular cliffs of Moher, and from the head of the pier, which shelters the tiny harbour, the view of the cliffs and the outlying islands is quite amazing whatever the weather, but maybe even more so on wild stormy days. But this is not one of those days, the sun is shining, the air is warm, and with the rug spread out on the soft grass we will be able to sit and admire the view as we listen to the waves gently lapping on the shore. Uncle has decided that he wants to stretch his legs, but the ladies are happy to seat themselves comfortably, and Grandma has wound the car window down so that she can join in the conversation. Oh no, I am not ready to sit down yet, and I take off after Uncle who is heading for the shore. This is a very small beach, but it is the only bathing area for miles around, and on this glorious sunny day it has attracted a lot of visitors some of whom are enjoying a swim. The idea of swimming doesn't appeal to me because I remember the day that Dad took my brothers and me to the river intending to teach us to swim. My eldest brother Tom had been on two other occasions, and he was to show us what to do. Dad was explaining the principles as we walked along, and said we only needed to remember the frogs we had watched in the pool on many occasions, and the way they moved their legs; he had already explained about the doggy paddle. It all sounded very interesting until we arrived at the riverbank. We were in our swimming costumes and watched as Tom jumped into the water, disappeared from our sight for a moment and then reappeared, gasping for breath before getting his arms and legs moving. That seemed OK, but then it was Joe's turn, and he was a bit hesitant until Dad said rather sternly, '*Jump*!' And so he did but, oh dear, that was a bit different kettle of fish. He disappeared but took much longer to surface than Tom had done, and then I thought he was going down again, and had forgotten Dad's instructions about moving his arms and legs until they all started moving at once. Then it was Patrick's turn and I sensed that he was even more hesitant than Joe, but Dad was waiting so he jumped in. At this point I thought, Oh, there won't be any more today! And I disappeared up the hill and down the lane as fast as my little legs would carry me.

'Oh, you've decided to come with me then!'

'Yes Uncle Ben, I know I should be listening to the next part of Aunt Alice's story but seeing you walking towards the beach I wanted to join you. Is that OK?'

'Oh, that'll be grand. Are you going to tell me what you see?'

'I'll try. Apart from the swimmers I can see people in the currach going to the Islands. Are they locals or fishermen?'

'This time they are neither because in the summer the currachs are used to take the visitors over to the Aran Islands as well.'

'What is there to see over there?'

'Well, the islands at one time would have been a peninsular extension of the Burren. At present they are considered to be the last outpost of Celtic culture and tradition, because the inhabitants speak only in the Gaelic language.'

'How do they survive over there because it looks so isolated?'

'Now, let's think, you know the Aran sweaters your Mum knits, well actually Aran knitting provides much of their livelihood, that and fishing.'

'Are there any people living on this little island close to us?'

'Oh, you mean Crab Island,' and he chuckles to himself as he says, *'the one you used to call Goat Island – no, it is deserted apart from birds and occasionally seals.'*

We have walked a short distance and are standing on the stony slope that leads down to a small area of sand, which is only exposed when the tide is out. Uncle watches as I wander over the stones, picking up a few that have caught my interest and I hand them over to him for safekeeping. There are pieces of wood that look very old and smooth, but Uncle says they look like that because they have been tossed about in the waves and battered on the shore. But he has now stretched his legs and wishes to rejoin the ladies. My eyes are still searching the stones, as we move away from the shore and suddenly I notice something unusual among the pebbles. When I pick it up I realise that, as well as some jagged edges, it has a smooth rounded corner with mouldings on it. Uncle Ben can't carry anything else but I showed it to him anyway, hoping he could tell me something about it, but his eyes light up at once and he says, *'How extraordinary! Well Aunt Alice will be delighted! Let's take it and show it to her.'*

The ladies are deep in conversation as we approach, but Aunt Alice stops as soon as she sees us coming and says to me, *'I thought you were desperate to hear the remainder of the story. What happened?'*

'I'm sorry Aunt, but when I saw Uncle walking towards the shore I wanted to join him in case the tide had left anything interesting on the beach.'

I hold out my hand and show her what I have found. She takes it from me, examines it carefully and says, *'Oh, I have to forgive you because this is a perfect visual aid for the next part of the story – aren't we lucky! And we can start right away but where do we begin? Oh yes, I may need your help with this Ben so you can both make yourselves comfortable.*

This is a piece from an old clay pot which looks as though it has been made on a potter's wheel and fired in a kiln.' As she examines the object more closely Aunt Alice says, *'We have no means of knowing how old it is, and that doesn't matter right now, because what I want to tell you goes back to how it might have all started with those ancient people long before the Celts came to Ireland. How do you think this object might have been made?'*

'Oh, I'm not sure but is it anything like making mud pies?'

'That's a wonderful answer, but for pottery like this you wouldn't use mud. It is a different material altogether called clay, which you won't find just anywhere, but there are certain low lying areas where there are rich deposits. We don't want to go into the geology of the subject right now, except to say that clay is a ductile, pliable material for making bricks and pottery, but the most important word, when thinking about clay is elasticity, but not the type you have in your garments. Perhaps it would be better to think of those times when you help your Mum to make rolls or scones. Have you noticed the difference between the two?'

'Oh, yes, scones are more solid and the rolls are squashy but spring back into shape.'

'That's exactly right, the rolls are springy because of the yeast that is used which makes the dough elastic, but more importantly it acts as a sort of glue which makes the flour tacky and holds it together.

Imagine for a moment how the ancient people would have started using clay to make pots. In order to do this we should go back to when people lived in caves. There would not have been the same distractions that there are today. For instance, you may not have many toys but they had none and books hadn't been invented. Remember what we have said about storytelling and using one's imagination, well imagine being seated around the fire in the cave or even out in the open. You know that looking at an open fire has a sort of magical feel about it; watching the smoke spiralling upwards and the flames flickering and changing colour from the deepest shades at the bottom to the lightest at the top. In this setting babies are lulled to sleep and older people like to reminisce and tell tales. They are truly beautiful moments.

We have already said that they were inventive, creative and productive people, and therefore would not sit idly looking into the fire for long periods of time; rather they would have wanted to use this time to make things.

Being hunter gatherers they would have been accustomed to collecting nuts, berries, herbs and edible seeds and roots; as well as kindling for the fire and straw or wild grasses, in fact anything suitable for making bedding. Now this is a lovely thought for all of us to explore, because we are all country folk. Their bedding would not have been made from bales of hay neatly tied in bundles; they would have used grasses, leaves or even twigs. They could use the twigs as a base or palette, and lay lots of grasses on top, but all things would have been at different stages of growth at different times of the year, and it is this we need to think about because plants, twigs and branches are all so bendy and pliable when young. While making up beds or feeding the fire they could be focused on what else they could do with these items. It is this 'what else' part which is good fun, and it also paves the way for useful items in the future. What sort of things might they have made?'

Mum, being so creative is in her element but Aunt Alice says, *'I know you Annie, you will leave us all standing with your answers because you are always doing things with your hands, so I am going to ask Ben to lead off with one idea they would have explored.'* Oh goodness, that's foxed him because he is not the sort of person who can work creatively with his hands. He definitely has an affinity with the hunting men who, on the whole, were responsible for making and maintaining the fires, not just for heating and cooking purposes but also as a safety measure. They knew that wild animals were afraid of fire and wouldn't come close as long as the fires were kept burning. So, his answer has to be, *'How about using the wood to keep the fire burning.'* Well, that lets him off the hook and of course I am sitting next to him and could see Aunt's eyes as she looks at me expectantly. For a moment I'm stumped, because she has asked me a question and I want to think carefully before answering, but that isn't easy with all the excitement. *'OK, I'm thinking about what I was doing this morning, because Dad and my brothers were working in the main vegetable garden, which is two meadows away from our house, and I had to take them their mid-morning drinks. I am used to walking round the edge of the meadows, because we are not allowed to walk on the grass until it has been cut. This is not a punishment for me, quite the opposite really, since the edges are full of flowers and change as the year moves on. I particularly like the tall wispy grasses with their delicate heads. My idea would be to use the rushes which I picked on my way back home, and sitting at the corner of the kitchen table, while Mum was making a cake for tea, I played and experimented with them, making knots and plaits and slitting some in order to push others through. Mum showed them to you all when you arrived, so I think the cave people would have experimented as I did this morning, but I don't think I made anything useful.'*

Aunt Alice says *'I know that's probably true, but you will use those ideas another time and no doubt then you will create something really useful.'*

Grandma is listening at the window of the car but is happy for Mum to be next. *'Oh, if I had the time I would be weaving with the fronds, hoping to make perhaps a table mat or maybe a covering for a stool, or even something to hang on the wall. There are endless, exciting possibilities but now Alice it is your turn.'*

'Well, this is my baby, this piece of pottery. It can't be difficult to imagine that the men out hunting would have come across areas of clay rather than mud. Clay could have stuck to their feet or footwear, and it would not have been as easy to remove as soil or even the mud you mentioned earlier, because it has that gluey quality. They might have picked up a lump of clay, taken it back to experiment with, but unlike your lumps of mud they would have discovered that being elastic and pliable it was possible to make many different shapes by pinching, plaiting, moulding or generally just fashioning into cups, mugs or plates, - anything useful. By the way I think you know what

a happy accident is! Your Mum has told me about your white blouse with the berry stain which you loved, but she needed to put more berry stains on it to make it look as though it had a pattern which was intended to be there. She then had to boil the blouse with some salt to set the colour, so that the pattern remained when the garment was washed. That was one type of happy accident for you, but your Mum didn't think so, because a happy accident really refers to something which was not intended, and which could have had an unhappy outcome, but in fact becomes something that has a positive result. In the same way those people may have left the shapes they had created close to the fire, or even tossed them into the embers if they weren't happy with what they had made, only to find when the fire died down that the discarded items had baked solid and had retained their shape.

That is a probable beginning to the story of pottery, but in order to produce something like the article you have found, something that would last and be durable, they would first have had to devise a means of reproducing and developing the heat generated from the fire, which could have reached much higher and more consistent temperatures. What I mean by this is your Mum's oven has a working temperature of about nine hundred degrees, but for firing pottery you need a consistent temperature of approximately four thousand five hundred degrees.

Of course, in the beginning they would have made all sorts of pots; the early ones would have been made entirely by hand, but to create the uniform shape of a pot such as this would have been, they needed to develop a means of turning the clay whilst using both hands to mould it into shape. Eventually the potter's wheel was developed for this purpose.

There is a very important lesson which we can all learn here, and I am so glad that you were able to collect your rushes this morning. It helps you and us to understand more fully an expression which some modern people use when referring to those ancients. The word is primitive and you may wish to explore this more fully when you are an adult, because of your own creative qualities, but right now we can say, even after thousands of years, there is no substitute for the beginnings of the creative process. The art of creative discovery can be playful and often messy, both mentally and, in the case of pottery, physically. We though can be very thankful that those early people learned to use the gifts they were born with. Those gifts, which they brought to Ireland were utilised to produce pottery, and this proved to be one of our main exports for a considerable time. Now who would like a cup of tea and one of Miss Murphy's delicious scones?'

Aunt came and put her arm around me, and said that there was a lot for me to think about before we examine the last question, which wasn't on my list but which would include all the spokes and the stories hopefully, and give me a strong centre for the Celtic wheel.

CHAPTER 13
THE CATHEDRAL AND THE LEGACY

Oh! Not only do we have our delicious scones and tea, but we also have Miss Murphy seated at our table; and this is a joyful occasion - friends catching up with each other. After some general chatter and conversation, Miss Murphy asks, *'Have you been doing anything special in the last few days?'* Oh dear! I know what they have been doing – taking me on a journey of a lifetime: taking me down memory lane: sowing seeds for the future, but most of all showing me that I can be a means of continuing the legacy, painting pictures in words for the future that many can enjoy. Oh, I hope I haven't exhausted them too much.'

As they continue to recount briefly the stories they have covered for Miss Murphy's benefit, I experience again a feeling of wonder and sense their enthusiasm in the retelling. Finally Miss Murphy asks the question, *'Why do you think Kilfenora Church was a cathedral?'* Grandma, being a member of that community, volunteers the answer, *'Well, for Àine's benefit, we should describe what a cathedral is, because she has been fascinated with all that she's seen there, and anyway that was probably where it all started.'*

Putting it very simply she goes on to explain, *'for all of our stories we have needed something to fire us. Now, St. Fachtnan, as we have mentioned already, founded the Church in the earliest years of Christianity in Ireland, almost as far back as the days of Saint Patrick. It became an Episcopal See in 1152, but why would it have been a cathedral? Well, to understand why, you must appreciate that it is not the building itself which is important, but the fact that a bishop was appointed to be there. The cathedra is not the building but the actual seat, which the Bishop sits on. The word cathedral was developed from the word for that seat, and because of that we believe that Kilfenora was of great importance in County Clare from the earliest times. Now we should ask ourselves the question, well why there?*

Some say that the Pope himself is in fact the Bishop of Kilfenora, and today the see is administered by the Bishop of Galway on the Pope's behalf.'

I haven't seen a picture of a Bishop yet, but I am wondering if he might look anything like the picture of St. Patrick, which I have in my Mass book. Mum has said that the tall hat is called a mitre; it has a tail at the back but I haven't asked her why. Looking like one of my triangles, and green in colour, it is outlined in gold with a gold strip up the centre. The gold band at the bottom of the triangle, which keeps it in place, is decorated in the centre with a little cross. There are two large spirals on either side of the centre strip – it looks so beautiful. The stick, or staff, which he is holding in the picture, is called a crozier, which also has a spiral at the top, and this spiral has a cross in the centre of it. Granddad told me that this is also called a shepherd's crook, because the Bishop is the shepherd of the flock. This image is so beautiful and, for a moment, I am lost in my own thoughts but then become aware that Grandma is looking at me very pointedly and, feeling guilty, I smile at her as she continues.

'There is unmistakeable evidence, of a powerful concentration of iron age people in this area, especially at Cahercaummaun. So we must ask ourselves the question, was this why Saint Fachtnan chose to build his church here? There is another large iron-age site at Ballykinvarga, about one mile to the east of Kilfenora, and there are sites even closer, including the Monk's Bed at Cill Chaimin.

If you were looking at a map of the Burren around the Kilfenora area, you would find many ancient sites marked there, including one not far from Lemeneagh Castle, called Templeline Church. And when you eventually visit this site you will find that although it is described as a church it appears to be closer in design to an iron-age enclosure. This could be the closest link we have with our Celtic, pre-Christian past, and the days when Christianity superseded paganism. We know that the early saints chose pagan holy sites on which to build their churches, and in the Burren there is much evidence of prehistoric people, especially in the remote high spots, such as at Poulnabrone. The landscape speaks of higher, holier things, and we can well imagine the human sacrifices of the Druids being practised in such places.

In the dark ages the survival of the people depended on being able to farm the land, and they will have chosen areas suitable for creating pasture land, where they could sow their crops; having first cleared the area of the forests and stones which existed in those days. Kilfenora is sufficiently close to both the very ancient sites and the farmlands further south.'

Although I am all ears and want to hear lots more, I have been aware over the for the past few minutes that Mum is becoming unsettled. She is not fidgeting as I do when I become restless, but I suspect that she has her mind on other things. I have realised that while we are all comfortable with our tea and scones, she is probably thinking about completing our evening meal, and will wish to be making her way back home. This will be more important to her than Kilfenora, because she is in the here and now rather than the past. Mum has a very gentle nature, and will not want to break up the party, so to make the point; I suppose I will have to be restless too. Most of the time this would be so easy for me, but not today! Perhaps, when everybody is well fed this evening, we will be able to continue our discussion. As we leave Miss Murphy smiling in the doorway, I think again, what a lovely angelic face she has.

No one has mentioned that this is to be Aunt and Uncle's last day with us, but I heard them tell Granddad on their first day that it would be a short break this time, because they hoped to return in the autumn. I think this change of normal routine must have something to do with Grandma but I don't want to ask any questions.

We have had such a happy time this afternoon in Doolin and now, as we return home, the adults chat light-heartedly about Miss Murphy and the days gone by. I know, though, that Mum still has a lot to do when we arrive home because her day started early in a frenzy of activity.

It may have been the activity in the kitchen, which wakened me so early, but I dressed quickly and finding Mum rushing about, I asked if I could be of any help to her. It gave me a lovely feeling inside when I heard her say, *'Thanks be to God for that',* and it sounds so much better than her usual comment, *'Oh my God, what have you done now'* – they may only be little accidents which I have, but someone has to be nurse and Mum is always so busy.

After I had eaten my porridge, Mum said *'Well dear, our first task is to find a duck.'* Oh Lord, why hadn't I stayed in bed and got up when the deed was done. It wasn't possible to say I don't feel well now, because I had just eaten a large bowl of porridge, and anyway she is relying on my help. So there is nothing for it and we headed for the yard, where the chickens, hens and ducks were busy scratching the soil and making such a cacophony, as Dad calls it, but I was used to the noise because I often fed them. I wanted to just stand and listen, but the young chickens, with their bright yellow, downy coats were simply asking to be picked up. Bending quickly I managed to catch one, which fitted so comfortably into the palm of my hand. The quiet cheep, cheep tugged at my heartstrings, and I was reluctant to let it go, but its mother was squawking loudly and looking at me intently. I just had to say sorry to her for the disturbance, because she is one of my favourites, and she usually tips her head from side to side when I am talking to her. But Mum had fixed her eyes on me too, because she had earmarked the duck chosen for our dinner. But first we needed to catch it!

When we had come into the yard, the increase in noise was one of expectation and excitement, because it would normally have meant that food was on its way. Last time there was this kind of uproar one of their number was to disappear under Mum's arm, destined for the pot, never to be seen again. On such occasions, are they aware of what is happening? They were not at all happy and I felt sad and guilty. The only consolation for them was that Mum had chosen a duck, which was limping badly and making more noise than the others, so you could almost say that it was a kindness after all. Even so, the struggle continued for some time, and the din became louder. At last, success! As we made our way out of the yard Mum said, *'You won't be happy about this part. I will see you in the kitchen shortly,'* but I was thinking of the birds that were waiting for their food; their noise a reminder that, not only had they been disturbed, but were angrily demanding that they be fed. I asked Mum if I could feed them and she said that I could. I was so glad of the distraction, not wanting to think about what was happening to the duck.

The noise outside soon died down; Mum was busily plucking the duck, whilst I held a bag open so that she could put the feathers in. These are saved and used for pillows or cushions at a later date. She then removed the innards of the bird, as it was now called, and saved the heart and gizzard, which would be boiled with the neck to provide liquid for the gravy. When the bird was cleaned, it was stuffed with a mixture she had prepared yesterday, using chopped sage, which I had collected from the garden: chopped onion: lots of breadcrumbs: beaten egg and some butter, and of course, salt and pepper. Having stitched up the opening to keep the stuffing in, she spread melted butter on top and put it in a roasting tin. Thankfully, I didn't have favourite ducks because this one had the promise of tasting really good.

The next task was to prepare the rhubarb pie, and I needed to collect the rhubarb from the garden – my least favourite task, since I am not allowed to take a knife. As the tug-of-war began, my patience soon gave way to grim determination, as I tried to pull the sticks from the base. Holding the stalk just below its enormous leaf allowed me to take a firm grip and then tug. Well the first stick was thin, but I used all my strength anyway; the stick came away easily but the momentum carried me on and I found myself upended on the leaves behind me. Thank goodness my brothers were still in bed! The next was a fat one but this time, exercising caution resulted in only half a stick. Well, the remainder would have to wait for an adult with a knife. After a lengthy battle with the rhubarb, there seemed to be enough for a pie or two. I struggled with the forest of leaves back towards the kitchen. On the way, I encountered Dad who had been to the main garden to dig potatoes and carrots. *'Who goes there?'* He asked. My indignation, which had been trying to find an outlet, now hits its target. *'It's me'* I shouted , *'I am not allowed to take a knife with me and nobody seems to know or care that my hands aren't strong enough to twist the leaves off, so I have had to bring them too.'* Trying to hide his laughter, but realising that this is a sensitive situation, he collected the rhubarb under one arm, and me under the other, and presented his bundles to Mum, who was preparing pastry. He could no longer contain his laughter and allowing me to stand on the floor; he proceeded to re-create the forest for her benefit. My indignation evaporated as I shared their amusement. He then found a knife and quickly lopped the leaves. Soon the pie was prepared and placed next to the duck. There was also ham, which has been soaking overnight – not everyone seems to like duck!

There was one more task for me and, as Mum prepared the potatoes and carrots, I returned to the kitchen garden to pick peas. No problems this time though, and when I returned she didn't seem to notice the one empty pod; newly picked peas taste delicious, cooked or uncooked, and even, or especially, at such an early hour. With most of the food preparation completed, we set the table in the dining room and, with a sigh of relief, closed the door. Everything was ready then for the evening.

Now arriving home, Mum's first task is to boil the kettle and be ready to make tea for the other family members, who have been working during the day, while we have been in Doolin.

The house is buzzing with chatter and it seems that everyone wants to talk at once. It is all a bit too much for Grandma who disappears to have a rest. I know Mum is thankful that she had made such progress this morning, and is now almost ready to serve the meal.

With so much happening, and knowing that Aunt and Uncle won't be with us again for some time, I am beginning to feel a little uneasy, because time is running out and they will soon be leaving. I remember Aunt's words in Doolin, when she said that there was a lot for me to think about before we examine the last question. I'm not too sure what she had meant by that. My personal questions were, 'Who am I? Where did I come from? How do I live and learn?' These aren't a problem for me now, because they have all been explained. They have also explained about the Celts too, except for the last question, and that was, what was their legacy? I wonder if they will have time for this but I really hope that Grandma doesn't need to go back to bed as soon as dinner is over.

The men have disappeared outside to have some quiet conversation, and take their drinks with them into the garden. Mum, who is a little hot and bothered, asks me to find the bell in Grandma's bedroom, and take it outside to ring, because she hasn't time to go chasing people! And didn't they know that dinner was almost ready!

Everyone, including Grandma, gathers quickly and makes their way to the dining room. Dad carves the meat, and soon we are all enjoying the result of Mum's sterling efforts this morning, and my humble contribution. Aunt Alice has managed to find proper ground coffee in Dublin – not the liquid in a bottle – and the aroma now fills the house. The men say they would like a tot in theirs. The boys wish to escape, so that they can play football with a few of their friends. Although I am allowed to taste the coffee, I don't care for it and have tea instead. Much to my relief Grandma seems to be fairly bright, but she may be reluctant to give way to tiredness, because she knows that Aunt and Uncle only have a short time left with us.

'We didn't finish our story this afternoon because Annie needed to return home, and what a beautiful meal she has provided for us, but I promised that we would try to fill in the centre of the wheel for the Celts before we go.' While she was still speaking, I wanted to rush up to Aunt and give her a big hug! As time is short, she very quickly tells the men what had been discussed in Miss Murphy's tearoom. Granddad looks at Grandma, with a smile, and I know that he doesn't wish her to be over-taxed. Looking at me he says, *'Well I can continue the story from here and ask for help if I have to. I understand that you still need to know about the high crosses and their interesting patterns, but before we go any further, there is an unusual but funny story we can tell you concerning the conversion of Ireland, without confusing you with too many historical facts. By the way, you do know what a fact is, don't you?'*

'Oh! I don't think anyone has told me about facts.'

'Well, a fact is something that actually happens. For instance, you go to bed each night and get up every morning unless you are ill. That is a fact.' Because he is smiling at me, and I don't want anyone to think about bed, yet, I have to say, *'Is it a fact that I ask too many questions, because Mum says I do, usually when she is too busy to answer them?'*

They all look at one another and laugh heartily. Granddad, still smiling, says, *'I think we can all say that you never stop asking questions, but perhaps we can agree that this is how you will learn. Indeed, you have been stirring our grey matter for the past few days, but that has been good for us too. Now though, let's look at a light-hearted story concerning the conversion of the Celts.*

This is music to my ears, especially as I now know what facts are; I realise that they have been giving me a lot of those, with the stories, and really they are much more difficult to remember, particularly if they have lots of names, dates and places. But I am not grumbling, because they have known this and given me many breaks in between. So I smile at Granddad and nod eagerly as he continues.

'We can think of the Celts as a nation of people, made up of many tribes, in all those countries where they first started, and where they eventually settled. Although the tribes may have differed in some respects, their beliefs and practices seemed to have been common to all. They had their own rulers, and teachers, poets and priests who were called Druids and they worshipped numerous gods. It took many years of training before the Druids were capable of fulfilling their many roles. One problem though was that they had an oral tradition, with nothing written down, which meant that they had to keep all of their knowledge in their heads; but this meant that they would eventually be able to pass this learning on to others. Because of this they achieved tremendous power and control over the people. The many different tribes in Ireland had their own chiefs, who were advised and guided by the Druids. Then along came St. Patrick, who brought with him a different type of teaching, and spoke about there being only one God – a God of forgiveness who was creator of all.'

Oh my goodness! How could one man hope to change so many people all by himself! What a challenge! I know from my own storybook how St Patrick came to Ireland. He lived in Britain and was abducted by Irish invaders. He was sold as a slave to a Celt who was a Druid, and forced to work as a shepherd. After six years in captivity he ran away, and walked over two hundred miles to board a ship and go back to his parents. The ship carried him to Gaul where he joined a Monastery and studied under St. Germanus in Auxerre. He had a dream in which he heard voices calling him back to Ireland. He asked the Pope for permission to go, and on arriving back in Ireland he found that Palladius was struggling with the conversion of the Irish people. When Palladius gave up the task and returned to Rome, Patrick was made Bishop of Ireland; this happened in 432 AD. He is supposed to have had a very special way with people and, knowing that he had a spiritual mission, prayed for strength to carry on even when people abused him. Granddad is laughing and speaking to me. *'What have you been thinking; you have had a far-a-way look on your face?'*

'Oh! I'm sorry Granddad, but when you mentioned St. Patrick, I couldn't help thinking of the challenge he faced in trying to convert all the people,' and I told him what I already knew.' He said, *'Your facts are right but he didn't use force to convert the Celts, and it didn't happen overnight or with the use of any magic power.*

We believe he arrived in Strangford Lough in County Down, where he soon converted a chief named Dichu who gave him a barn, which he consecrated as his first church. Some time later he made his way towards the Hill of Tara, Co. Meath. This was the seat of the High King of Ireland, whose name was Laoghaire. This was when he had his first major encounter, because having arrived at Slane at the time of the Easter Vigil he lit his fire there. The King had ordered that all fires be extinguished before the new fire was lit at Tara. When they saw Patrick's fire, the Druids warned the King that unless it was put out it would burn for ever. The King asked who had lit this fire against his orders. The Druids, who had already felt threatened by St. Patrick, were happy to tell the King who it was. Patrick was summoned by the King, and as he journeyed with his followers they recited The Lorica.

'Oh Granddad, what is the Lorica, and can we say some of it now?'

'Well The Lorica is another name for St. Patrick's breastplate and it is also called the Hymn of St. Patrick. It is long and beautiful, but we tend to say only the last part, which we call our breastplate. I think you should know all of that part, so we'll all say it together!'

Christ with me, Christ before me, Christ behind me,

Christ in me, Christ beneath me, Christ above me,

Christ on my right, Christ on my left,

Christ where I lie, Christ where I sit, Christ where I rise,

Christ in the heart of every man who thinks of me,

Christ in the mouth of every man who speaks of me,

Christ in every eye that sees me,

Christ in every ear that hears me.

I arise today through a mighty strength, the invocation of the Trinity,

Through belief in the threeness, through confession of the oneness

Towards the Creator.'

Granddad continues,

On reaching Tara there followed a confrontation between St. Patrick and the Druids, and through God's mighty power, Patrick prevailed. The King was so impressed that he gave Patrick freedom to carry on with his work, and he himself became a convert to Christianity.

There are many accounts of St. Patrick's work: some will be true and others invented. There is one particular story, which we believe to be true, it is also sad, but you I believe will think it rather funny. Now I'm going to ask you to imagine St. Patrick standing here with us; you are a pagan King who is going to be baptised, and you are standing in front of him.'

'Oh, I would like to pretend, but I have been baptised already!'

'We know that, but then you were a baby, this time you are pretending to be a King; in fact the King of Munster and your name is Aengus.'

'I would really like that. Does everyone have to obey the King and can he have everything he wants?'

'Not always, and you are only pretending remember, so it will be bed at the usual time. Now St. Patrick has just finished sprinkling holy water on you, he gives you his blessing and raises his crozier and thumps it down firmly onto the ground, declaring that you are a Christian. You though, happen to be standing too close to him and the point of the crozier goes through your foot instead.'

'Oh I can't stay still and I have to hop around, it's bad enough when I accidentally stub my toe! Please tell me this is not a true story!'

Aunt Alice is laughing now, as I continue hopping around. *'The story is true, the funny part is, when St. Patrick saw what he had done, he asked the King why he didn't cry out, and the King replied that he thought it was all part of the ceremony.'*

'Oh you were right when you said it was sad and funny; I'm glad we are only pretending.' Granddad says, *'You see, Kings don't always get exactly what they want! All this happened at Cashel, in Co. Tipperary, which was the seat of the King of Munster. St. Patrick's high cross, which is erected there is a reminder of what happened. But talking about this cross takes us back to our own unfinished story about the high crosses in Kilfenora. First though I think your foot needs a rest, and maybe you could help your Mum make us all a nice cup of tea.'*

As we drink our tea Granddad says that we can now continue with the story of Kilfenora. *'I want to say that the Cathedral is very famous for the high crosses that we have seen there, and perhaps we could consider how and why they were made. We can assume that the earliest crosses will have been very simple markers, indicating meeting places or places of Christian worship, possibly developed from the standing stones and such like, which could also have marked places of pagan worship. The large stones, so readily available throughout the Burren, would have originally been carved with simple pictures and symbols of Christian belief. It is thought that the pagans worshipped the stones themselves. The kings of Scotland and England where crowned on sacred stones, and still are to this day in Westminster Abbey in London. Even the famous King Arthur drew the mystical sword Excalibur from such a stone. Although the story of the sword and the stone is probably in the realm of myth and legend, the fact that it is so well known around the world emphasises the importance that has been placed on such stones. Here in Ireland the Celtic High Kings were chosen at the Stone of Destiny, on the Hill of Tara.*

We can say that the pagan beliefs regarding stones were converted to the true faith by the early saints, in the same way that the pagan religious sites were used as places of Christian worship, except that the stones themselves were not worshipped only used as symbols. The pagans had worshipped water at the many wells and springs throughout Ireland, and these too were consecrated as places of veneration – not the water itself, but the God of creation who had given the wells so freely and in such abundance.'

Oops! This is a long way from my first visit to Kilfenora and what a lot I have to think about but before I can gather my thoughts Granddad is off again. *'I wonder,'* he says, looking at the others, as though I had gone to bed already '*Do you think she might be interested in hearing about the wells*?' This time it seems as though he wishes to go in a completely different direction. Well he can't go very far or for very long, because Grandma is beginning to nod off and the way things are going she'll be in bed before me. Aunt, who must be thinking about her packing, turns to Granddad and says *'It really must be brief because we need to be getting back to our hotel, in Lisdoonvarna. Are there any special wells on the road to Lisdoonvarna?'* In reply Granddad says, *'Not if you take the most direct route, but of course there is St. Senan's Well at Kilshanny. The most significant well in these parts lies on the road between the Cliffs of Moher and Liscannor; it is called St. Brigid's Well. She was possibly the most famous of Irish saints after Saint Patrick and travelled the length and breadth of Ireland in a chariot, carrying on the work, which he had started. Brigid was a founder of monasteries and a worker of miracles. As a child she showed great generosity, to the point of giving away her mother's butter supplies to feed the poor, and even her father's sword for the same purpose. On becoming a nun she was ordained a bishop by accident – or some would say by God's design, setting a precedent for much later controversy surrounding the roll of women in the church. She is credited with having converted a dying king on his deathbed by weaving a plaited cross of rushes as she prayed, which later set the tradition of making Saint Brigid's crosses on the First of February each year, in her memory, and in the hope that households would be protected throughout the year.'*

Not wishing to distract Granddad from his story, but desperately needing to know, I cannot help but say *'Weaving, weaving! Oh, I was trying to weave with my rushes this morning. Do we make our own, because I've never seen anyone doing it?'*

He answers, *'Yes we do, you're usually in bed, but next year you should be able to help your Mum. She uses six bunches of rushes, in groups of three. They are interwoven in such a way that the ends are tied together to form a simple cross like those you have seen. There is never a shortage of rushes to make them, as you know; they grow in every field and byway hereabouts. And now Young Lady it really is time for bed.'*

CHAPTER 14
HAZEL NUTS

This is a beautiful early October morning and over breakfast Mum says, '*Since you don't have anything organised for this morning and the sun is shining, I think you should make this your day for a visit to the hazel scrub. We will need nuts for the first winter celebrations.*' Oh, I can feel the excitement creeping in at the thought of our yearly nut-picking expedition. It is hard to describe the taste of those freshly picked hazel nuts, but my brothers enjoy them as much as I do and they are now as eager as I am to be going. It doesn't take long to finish breakfast and get organised. Our school satchels are perfect for this trip, because they were made to carry lunch boxes as well as books, and they also have a big pocket for plimsolls and gloves or other necessities. The most important thing about them, when we use them for nut picking, is that we are able to adjust the straps and wear them as the horse wears his oats bag over his neck. We have to be able to wear them like this, so that our arms are free to climb and to reach out for the nuts, and anyway it's easier to feed them into the bag. It is so frustrating, when grabbing a cluster of over-ripe nuts, to have to watch them fall from the husk and get lost in the undergrowth.

When we're ready, and with a snack in each satchel and a bottle of orange squash entrusted to Tom, who is the eldest, and in charge, we set out with Mum's words to be careful ringing in our ears. We enter the field across from our home and set off down the steep hill, passing through two more fields before reaching the hazel thicket. There is still a feeling of wonder as we look at this dense collection of bushes covered in leaves. We didn't have any trouble coming through the fields, because we could see the stones and the uneven ground, and we could see the cow pats too and were careful not to tread on them. We have been chattering happily on the way, mostly in a competitive spirit guessing who will fill their satchel first; but standing at the entrance to the coppice we experience a change in our mood and become thoughtful. Granddad had told us last year about some of the history concerning the hazel trees – we asked why they grew in this particular area, but were not found in any of the fields near our home. He had said that the nature of this bush was to spread and spread if it wasn't controlled. It was one of the trees which covered the whole of Ireland, with the Yew, the Oak and the Pine, in ancient times. In order to create pasture land areas needed to be cleared, and they remained free of shrubs as long as grazing continued. But the uneven stony ground in some areas made it very difficult to clear, and this was one such area. He had also told us that the hazel tree was one which the Celts considered to be sacred, and in their time cutting one down could mean death. The wood from this tree was one of the main materials used in building their homes. It was also used to make fencing, and special pieces were cut to make divining rods to find underground water. Granddad had also said they still use them in some places today, but I hardly think it would be necessary here with all the rain we get in Ireland now.

This had been a very interesting story but at this moment we are more concerned with the thought of entering the darkness. At least I am, because the coppice is dense with very little light, and these trees have grown on the very rocky ground of a downhill slope.

Back in the spring, when we visited the farmhouse in the valley below on an errand, we could see the layout of the land because the hazel bushes shed their leaves in the autumn. We had been excited then when we saw all the male catkins, which were long and brightly coloured, being a mixture of pale brown and yellow. The female catkins were mostly hidden in buds and had deep, deep pink flowers. We noticed the new hazel trees which were beginning to shoot, and there was a promise of a wonderful harvest. Of course all that happened before the leaves appeared and now it seems very dark in there. The scene is so different, there are so many leaves which tend to hide or shield the nuts. The excitement is really in finding and picking that first cluster.

The boys are very enthusiastic, but why do I feel so hesitant when I have always been at least as daring as they are. My brother Tom, focussing his gaze on me, tells us that we must all stay close together and not go "wandering off". Oh goodness that has started it. My mind takes off on a "what if" journey. Realising that my brothers have not been included in the summer stories about the ancients, and having decided to tell them during one of our long winter evenings, I now feel at a disadvantage. This is not the time to share with them, and nor is it possible to say how I feel. For just a few short moments, which seems like an eternity, I am back in the time of those early inhabitants, who would have faced whole forests such as this; forests of trees and brambles which somehow they managed to clear. They were not put off by the challenge because their survival depended on it. Oh Heavens, imagine coming face-to-face with one of them in there – in the darkness! Heaven forbid! They have my respect and my gratitude for the legacy they have left us, but I really don't want to meet them right now!

'Well, are you coming or not?' Tom's voice is sounding just a little impatient, and he has already started to penetrate the thicket, followed closely by Joe and Pat.

A few giant leaps for me and I shout, *'Yes, I'm right behind you,'* and I resolve to stay as close as possible. Looking upwards I spy the first cluster of nuts with the light reflecting on the hard shells. Gone is my resolve to be better than good. My whoopee would have alerted any Celts that might have been there, and I was about to inflict the first graze on my knee while trying to leap and hang on to the hazel branch.

The boys come rushing back, and seeing me examine my leg, they have no qualms in saying, *'It serves you right.'* But then Tom, who is very protective says, *'OK, if you must pick it I will pull the branch down, but next time call me first!'* Laughing and trying not to think about my damaged knee, I agree. Anything, if only I can hold my find in my hand for a few moments before releasing the nuts from the husk.

For me the excitement has nothing to do with the challenge made earlier about who will be first to fill their satchel, rather it is the joy on seeing the first fruit that has developed from those catkins we have seen in the spring. This has to be a miracle of creation.

There are four nuts in this cluster. Of course some of the others can have as many as five. Thankfully these nuts are not over ripe or they would have fallen as we picked them, but they remain firmly encased in their bright green, slightly spongy husks, with only the tips peeping out. Removing them is no problem and now they rest in the palm of my hand. They feel so smooth – soft to the touch, despite having a hard outer shell. They vary in colour too, and although they are all a deeper shade at the base, the overall colour itself is called hazel.

We are always amazed when we see the number of bushes, but find that when we start to search for the nuts there are so few on each bush; those that are there are cleverly hidden by the leaves, and so it becomes a feat of discovery on every tree.

We work very well for the first hour or so but, on finding an open rocky space, we all agree that it is time for a break. We are also in agreement that we can't resist what we are going to do next. It isn't discipline which has stopped us attempting to crack some nuts as soon as we pick them, but the lack of room in the undergrowth. Now we have each found a small stone, and placing the nuts on a large flat rock we attempt to crack them open. So much for discipline; having two nuts fit for eating, Pat's and mine are shattered beyond recognition. A swift demonstration from Tom shows that if we want to eat the kernel in the centre we must use care when hitting the shell. Our patience is rewarded when we finally manage to crack the nut and taste the first fruit of the season. It would be so easy to stay and gorge ourselves but these nuts are supposed to be our Halloween and Christmas treats. So, with a promise of more to come during the festivities, we have just a few and quickly eat our sandwiches, have a drink and return to our task.

We need to leave some room in our satchels, as they will quickly be filled when we arrive at our second destination, because this is really a dual expedition. Working steadily for another hour, we feel that our combined efforts will be sufficient for everyone's needs, and we can now continue downhill, skirting the edge of the coppice, until we arrive at the stone wall surrounding the orchard in the valley. A quick look over the wall reveals a feast of bright rosy apples just waiting to be picked. Oh my, this is a temptation too great to resist; and climbing quietly and carefully over the wall, we approach the trees furthest from the house. The two older boys quickly climb them, but Pat and I stand underneath ready to catch the apples as they drop. It doesn't take long to fill the remaining space in the satchels, and feeling that we are unobserved we secure the flaps, but oh dear, we hear a voice nearby, and suddenly realise that the lady of the house has been watching and enjoying our furtiveness. She says in a kind, laughing voice, *'There are lots more, and I have a spare bag! When you've finished, there is some tea and scones waiting for you.'* Tom, being older, seems slightly uncomfortable when we are discovered, but the remainder of us are not really old enough to worry, and the sound of tea and scones is music to our ears. Of course this lady knew all about our annual trip to the Oughtdarra Orchard, and was more or less expecting us. Our only embarrassment was knowing that she will have fun sharing all this when she next sees our parents.

Autumn is always a very special time on the farm, and particularly here in the Burren. There is a sense of relief that harvesting is complete. The peat is stacked high near the house, which will provide warmth and fuel for cooking. The hay, which provides some of the animal food, is stored under a huge tarpaulin which protects it from the worst of the weather. The potatoes, swedes and turnips are stored in a mixture of straw and peat, which will preserve them until they have been used up. Mum has made bramble jelly, blackberry jam and rhubarb jam, and the jars are neatly stored in the cupboard. Nuts and apples have been collected too in readiness for the celebrations, but what a pity we can't save the mushrooms. Collecting blackberries in September means combining it with mushroom picking, and for this we need to take two containers. It also means going out early in the morning if we wish to collect the mushrooms while they are really fresh. They are always at their best when the weather is wet or even after a very heavy dew and you can be sure to find them in the meadow because the animals fertilise the fields and there is no problem in filling a large container. It is really exciting when we come across a circle of mushrooms which we call fairy rings. The whole family enjoys them, but oh, what a treat when the gatherers are allowed to sprinkle a few of them with salt, standing them on the range until the heat has melted the seasoning, when they are ready to be eaten.

Although gathering the mushrooms is fun, the same cannot be said about picking blackberries in these same conditions. The spiders love to weave their webs between the bramble branches, and the webs catch the rain or the dew drops. It is very difficult trying to avoid being showered when reaching for the larger berries, which always seem to be at the top of the bush. Spider's webs and misty mornings are part of nature's cycle, and as Granddad says, 'All things which grow and produce fruit must also rest awhile.' As the trees and plants prepare to settle down, they provide one last glorious display of colour, which changes day by day until the leaves fall from the trees and join the decaying undergrowth. But the evergreen trees, shrubs, holly and ivy seem to take on a new lustre, and stand out sharply against the decaying foliage, and against the greys and browns of the rocks and stones.

By the time Halloween arrives, the daylight hours have become shorter, and we are preparing to spend more time indoors. I remember our summer stories, when I learned that Halloween is really a legacy from the Celts; one of their main celebrations to mark the end of summer and the beginning of their New Year. It was a time when they celebrated the living and the dead.

Well, it seems that for us it is a little different. Yes, we know that the first of November is All Saints Day, and the second is All Souls Day, when we will be at Mass praying for so many people who have died, but tonight is different. It is fun but scary too; all the ghost stories we have been listening to when we are really supposed to be in bed, simply adds to the scariness. Jack-o-the-lantern and the banshee seem to have more meaning tonight. There are also those unsettled spirits we hear about, which are supposed to appear on this night, oh and then there is the true story which we overheard not so long ago. One evening the visitors were chatting about the ancient sites, such as the forts, the barrows and the cairns, which are believed to be ancient burial grounds and shouldn't be tampered with. Our visitor told the story of the men who ignored this advice, and on one isolated occasion, after a visit to the pub, decided to investigate what was really in the fairy mounds. Having collected some spades and dug in the dead of night they were scared witless, so the story goes, and ran screaming all the way home. Since that day their family hasn't prospered. Indeed, we children won't be found wandering out of the house tonight. And to make matters worse there will only be one well lit room in the whole house, where everyone will be gathered, and we will have to use a candle if we wish to visit any of the other rooms. Heavens, couldn't we be allowed to have lamps in all the rooms on a night like this; using candles reminds us of our own spooky games when we use material and our fingers to make shadows on the wall, with appropriate noises to boot. But we are told that it is traditional to have candles lit as a sign of respect for the dead. The only consolation is that we won't need to leave the room until it is time for bed, and right now it's time to enjoy the fun. The most popular game is apple dunking, or apple bobbing; we must place our hands behind our backs and retrieve an apple from a bowl of water using only our teeth. After this it is time to have a few games of rings. The ring board is made in the shape of a shield which has thirteen numbered hooks on it. The player must stand a certain distance from the board, and using a set of five rubber rings, throw them one at a time attempting to lodge them on the hooks. The winner is the one with the highest score. We all enjoy this game and, as the adults tell us, it is good for our sums, but only if we manage to get the rings on the hooks! Fortunately the younger ones are allowed to stand closer to the board.

The most important part of the evening though, is listening to the adults reminiscing about their own childhood as we sit around the fire, eating nuts and biscuits, made by Mum, followed by hot chocolate and then bed, because we will need to be up early as tomorrow is All Saints Day. But with all the talk about ghost stories and the dead this was one night when we children all wanted to share the same bed.

November seems to be a month of decay, when all the leaves underfoot have withered and become tacky in the damp atmosphere. As time passes they return to the soil and the ground is clear again. From now until the end of February we can all expect to have a cold or flu, or some other ailment, and of course Grandma is not well, and Mum will be run off her feet again; but she makes beautiful beef broth and carrageen blancmange, which are her standby remedies for all recovering patients.

Back in the spring, and before the farm and the peat took up too much of his time, Dad reminded us that we should collect the carrageen and, as he said, 'we are lucky to be able to collect our own;' travelling to Poulsallagh Bay, which is only a few miles from Rockville, provided an opportunity to ask him why this was so. We used the horse and cart for this journey and he was able to give us his undivided attention until we arrived, and anyway the horse seemed to know where it was going.

Dad told us we were very lucky because carrageen doesn't grow in all coastal areas but mainly in those parts surrounded by the Atlantic Ocean. Some people call it moss or seaweed, and it grows among the rocks and can only be gathered when the tide is low and the rocks exposed. Although it is called carrageen, which is the Gaelic name for Irish Moss, it isn't really a moss at all but a type of seaweed which looks like curly grass and it floats in the rock pools. There is no problem finding it because the vibrant green, purple, red and yellow colours make it stand out clearly, especially when the tide has just gone out.' When I reminded him that I had eaten some last year, he said that it is particularly good when fresh, but that we must take it home and dry it so that it could be stored until your Mum needed to use it. It has always been a nourishing food and during the famine it helped to keep many people alive. But we only use it if someone has been ill and unable to eat for a time. And, of course, it is very good for coughs and stomach problems. I remember Mum giving us children more than usual last year when we all had whooping cough. She had boiled it in milk and, after straining it, she added dark brown sugar to the liquid, leaving it to set and become cold. She explained at the time that carrageen has a gelling affect, and could be used in soups and gravies; in fact in any liquid which needed to be thickened.

We children love blancmange with brown sugar because it has a toffee flavour. When we asked about the brown sugar we were told that the molasses was good for us. The animals were given molasses and nuts when there was a shortage of hay. It was a rare treat for all of us to be given something which was both good for us and had a yummy taste!

CHAPTER 15
THE FUNERAL

1947 has been a very special year for me, and I seem to have grown not just in height, but in my understanding of things and how they are. Throughout the summer holidays Uncle Ben and Aunt Alice have made two visits from Dublin, and they came again in the autumn. Although they stayed in the hotel in Lisdoonvarna, they spent many happy hours with us. They took Grandma out for short drives when she felt well enough to go. These days she doesn't wish to travel in the pony and trap, but now, here we are in September, and it is such a lovely warm day, and Granddad says that he would like to take her to Fanore beach, if Dad can drive them, because he doesn't think there will be another day like this.

The trap is large enough to seat four people comfortably, and I am allowed to go with them. I think it is very unusual that Granddad is asking anyone to drive, because this is something he loves to do himself, and he looks so masterly when he is holding the reins and guiding the pony. So there is just the four of us, and it doesn't take too long for me to realise that this is to be a very special journey for my grandparents. They sit side by side, with a rug draped over their knees, and I know that under the rug they are holding hands. Dad and I, who are seated on the other side, don't need a rug as he is busy concentrating on his task, and being so inquisitive, I am looking at the beautiful colours all around now that autumn is here. But we know that this journey is about the two people who are seated opposite us, looking sad at times, and then laughing a little, but mostly they are quiet and peaceful. Without understanding the reason it seems important for me just to be there with them.

Mum has packed tea and biscuits, and when we arrive I am able to help in setting up the drinks; having alighted from the trap it is possible to put the tray on the seat. When Dad and I finish our drinks he says we should have a short walk. Granddad and Grandma have no intention of leaving the trap, and simply need a little time to themselves to reminisce, as this has always been their "special place". Dad has tethered the pony to a large rock and she stands grazing contentedly in the warm sunshine. As always my heart seems full when I am here at Fanore, rather than standing outside Rockville looking down towards the sea. Will I ever be able to find the right words to describe what I see? Listening to the adults attempting to describe this area makes me so aware that they, even in their older years, cannot manage it either. Being young doesn't seem to matter in this sense; it is, as Granddad has said earlier in the year, a place where one has "to be". And being is all I can hope to achieve, since doing means walking, whilst watching every step. This is very rocky ground, which looks as though someone has used the icing knife to smooth out every little bump, and the result looks like a gigantic iced cake with cracks in the icing. It has been here for millions of years, and the rain has penetrated the limestone pavement and carved out fissures and grykes, which in time have filled with sediment, where seeds have found a home when blown in from the Continent on the Atlantic breeze. Now there is mostly the remains of what has been a feast of colour and variety throughout the spring and summer. Back then there was such an uncontrollable urge to sing and dance on the larger flat stones, but also to lie down where the stone had soaked up the heat from the sun – it felt so smooth and warm almost like a giant bed. For children and adults it is always the same at such times, everyone seems quiet, simply wanting to soak up the spirit of the scene – not really believing but hoping it won't just go away. Those were the wonderful sunny memories of a place that seems to breathe its spirit into a body. Even I know that rock is supposed to be a dead substance, but there is a problem accepting this, because it appears to have a strength of its own and to transfer it even when it's being lashed by storms and huge waves. Now though, there is a feeling of vastness and gentleness, breathing peace with each wave which laps upon the shore.

Nature has provided a flat grassy area in the midst of all the stone, and this is where the trap is parked. The two people inside are able to enjoy the whole scene and remember. All of their married life has been spent within a short driving distance of Fanore, they have brought their children here for picnics just as my Dad does with our family.

Dad and I walk for about half an hour, not saying much, but he comments that this is a special time, as Grandma probably won't be able to come here again. It makes me feel sad, but we all know that she is spending more time in bed these days, and on those occasions we children mustn't be too boisterous when playing indoors. There is also a sense of gladness deep inside, because this has to be the most perfect place for a person to feel a sense of timelessness, and being told that eternity is also a vast and wonderful place, it is possible to feel that going there is not a cause for worry.

Our arrival back at the trap seems to go unnoticed, because they are huddled very close together and lost in their own world. They have had their time in their own place and now seem very peaceful. They brighten when they see us and say that it is time to go home for tea. What a beautiful ride home, listening to the birds singing in tune, with the clip clop of the pony's hooves, and feeling the gentle rhythm of the trap. I could be lulled to sleep, and when I look at Grandma I realise that she has given way to this blissful moment, as Granddad chats quietly to Dad about some of the chores to be done at home.

When we arrive home, Grandma says that she is very happy to have been on this special trip so late in the year, but is content and retires early. Granddad seems very thoughtful as the evening passes.

The beautiful weather continues for about a week, and then it becomes colder and the days are much shorter. We have our usual Halloween celebrations and our evening pastimes, which we call our winter games, but they are all a little subdued this year, because even when Grandma gets up during the day, she is always back in bed before tea, and very often says she doesn't need any food. The house is always busy though, with many visitors coming to pay their respects and wishing to know how she is. When she is not able to meet them, they still stay for a cup of tea and a chat, and of course it is good that Granddad is able to talk to old friends, who understand these things, because as they often say, 'Well, it's like this', and we know that they have had similar experiences. Mum is often rather harassed; now she is being a nurse as well as a Mum, and we try to be on our best behaviour.

The preparations for Christmas are different from the usual noisy bustle, and something seems to be missing somehow. Although as children we notice the lack of excitement, since we are often the cause of it, we can't fail to be aware of the subdued whispers, whenever someone goes to check on Grandma. The Doctor comes every few days and chats quietly for a while afterwards, sometimes having a cup of tea with Granddad because they have been friends for a long time.

Christmas arrives and it's different again; we are too young to attend Midnight Mass, and getting up as early as we need to, on Christmas morning, makes it feel as though we are going to Midnight Mass anyway. No breakfast, no food, but when we arrive at Church, there is all the mystical mystery there, with the crib and the decorations, and the candles. It is here too that we can pray for all those who can't be with us, and particularly for those who are seriously ill. I hear Grandma's name mentioned, and know that for a while it is possible to let go of the heartache, which seldom leaves me these days, particularly when I look at Granddad, whose step has become slower as though he is carrying a heavy weight on his shoulders. He is not able to be with us on this occasion, needing instead to be on hand at home. I feel that all the prayers being said can reach them there, leaving me free to experience the total joy of this moment. We are always being told that a mystery is something which can't really be experienced, and this has to be the greatest mystery; one which doesn't need to be explained. It simply needs to be felt deep inside, where it flows into all the aching spaces, leaving them full of wonder and joy.

When we return from Mass, Granddad looks at me and says, *'I know you haven't eaten yet, but Grandma would love to see you, as she is sitting up this morning. You can take your porridge through and sit on the bed, so that you can tell her everything before you open your presents.'*

'Oh Granddad, being able to be at Mass has been the best present of all! Can I tell her that?'

He nods and says, '*Yes, just tell her what is in your heart. I think that is what she really needs to hear now.*' Seeing her sitting up in bed looking so frail, I am no longer in awe of her, and remember how she and Granddad had been in the trap at the seaside. I want to be close to her and share my beautiful moments. When I finish my porridge, I look at her face and realise that there are tears on her cheeks. I've been given a napkin in case of accidents, and ask if I can dry her tears, but then she says she needs a hug too. Now I know that the magic and mystery of Christmas is really working; I also sense that she will not be here for another Christmas. Then she seems to brighten, and with a beautiful look on her face, which we haven't seen for some time, she declares to everyone's amazement that she would like to join us all for lunch. Mum is happy too and relieved because she doesn't need to prepare a special tray, and so we are all feasting together just like other years. Grandma eats only a few morsels, but remains bright and chatty throughout; staying with us for a few hours, until she says that she needs assistance to go back to bed.

Over the next week her condition deteriorates, and by the beginning of the New Year the Doctor is coming in daily, and then twice a day. Finally it's just a matter of hours. We are all asked to go into her room to say a quiet prayer, and then at last we hear Granddad say, '*She's gone.*' Life is not going to be the same again.

This is my first experience of family bereavement. Grandma has been a wife, mother and grandmother, and there are many tears shed, but soon all the adults dry their tears for there are so many practical arrangements to be made. The most urgent need is to let the local ladies know, because some have said that they would be available to help Mum to lay out the body; and because she knows that it is important for me to be aware of what's happening, she explains that it is necessary to wash and change Grandma, and have her laid out with clean sheets; but she also says that I should wait until they have finished and then go in to see her.

How very different she seems now with just a white sheet over her, having her hands clasped on her chest with rosary beads draped over them. Her face has always been pale but now it looks like white marble, and even though her eyes are closed she looks so peaceful. I can imagine her guardian angel sitting on her shoulder, even though I know her spirit has gone on its way to heaven.

The days are now extremely busy, almost like the run up to Christmas, but for different reasons. Relatives have been notified by telegram and have begun to arrive. There are endless visitors who come to pass on their condolences. One of the first tasks has been a visit to town to buy a plentiful supply of drinks and food. I have not seen a barrel of porter before, and wonder if I might be able to find a spoon and test the tap when no one is looking. When someone helps himself without concentrating on what he is doing I change my mind; the liquid flows over the rim of his glass and spills into the container, which Mum has fortunately provided for such accidents. Well it was just a thought, and anyway I'm kept very busy opening the door when people arrive, and of course the kettle is permanently on the boil. Even though the occasion is a sad one, the atmosphere is almost one of celebration and reunion, as people catch up with one another, because some have come from overseas and haven't been here for some time.

Although we children know that this particular time is referred to as "the wake", we have not experienced it before and everything is very strange and different. The adults are not really being themselves, and there are times when I know they would wish to be alone, but it isn't possible; they have become tired with all the arrangements and the waiting. We children don't understand what we are waiting for, and it isn't a good time for questions, so we will have to wait too. In the meantime we have difficulty coping with what is a very unreal situation.

Each day we pop in to be with Grandma and say a prayer, but as the days go by it becomes even more difficult and more unreal. We don't want to be there by ourselves, and we can't really ask any of the adults, so we go in together, but somehow this seems to make it more difficult to say any prayers. We all know about the spirit leaving the body, but no one has prepared us for this time, coping with a cold, motionless figure, and knowing her as we have, we all half expect her to sit up in bed and reprimand us for our bad behaviour, especially when, due to our ignorance and a certain sense of fear, we just want to giggle. We hope none of the adults find us in this very disrespectful state, but their behaviour seems just as odd. It almost seems easier to kneel by our beds at the end of the day and pray for her there, because as time goes by we are not happy even passing the open door of her bedroom.

There is a sense of relief when the funeral day arrives. It is a very cold, damp, grey January day, and there is a different type of bustle; all the adults, except Mum, are dressed and ready for Church. The hearse and the Priest arrive at the same time – the Priest blesses "the remains", and then we are allowed to go and say goodbye to our Grandmother. I thought this would be easy, because I have already done this on the first day, but Granddad has remained by the coffin, and seeing his face my composure disappears, because I know that he has realised that he won't see her again in this life, and my wish is to make all the sadness go away so that he can look happy again.

Shortly afterwards the coffin is in the hearse and it has started to move slowly down the hill from our house. So many people have arrived to follow the cortege, but Mum remains at home so that she can prepare a hot meal for family members when they return. Now she stands with us children at the gate and watches for a long time, until they have all disappeared from our view. Our tears flow freely now; this seems so final. Even the weather being so miserable and damp seems to match the occasion; but it is doubly hard for me to come to terms with all that has happened. I know that her spirit will be happy, and remember instead that beautiful time that she and Granddad had shared in Fanore, when they must have been preparing themselves for this day; a memory which Granddad would always treasure; and I am so happy that I was part of it.

CHAPTER 16
THE GOOSE

Easter seems to be looming very quickly this year. I know it can vary on a three-week cycle over the years, but I can't understand why, even when my parents try to explain. Perhaps when I am older it will be easier to understand. The fact is that this year it is going to be at the end of March, but I think it is so much better when it falls during the second week of April. I think I shall ask my parents to explain to whoever who is responsible for setting the date for Easter, that the middle of April would be wonderful!

In April it seems that all the earth, the plants and the trees are coming back from the dead, or at least from hibernation and they want to shout, 'We're here! Let's get going!' And they do, taking all living creatures with them. The hibernating animals in their burrows uncurl themselves from their winter sleep, and edge towards the light and sniff the air, which no doubt smells really good. The warmth encourages them to emerge and prepare for another season. The horses raise their heads and whinny loudly, as they fill their lungs with air, and sensing the changing season, they cannot contain themselves. It is something that only horses do, for no apparent reason they just take off as though they have been stung by a bee. You couldn't imagine a cow doing that! It is so funny watching them take off at a gallop, every now and then, kicking their legs into the air as far as they possibly can. The gallop becomes a race which lasts for quite a while and when they come to a standstill, they sniff the air again and continue to graze contentedly as though it had never happened. Even if there is only one horse it follows the same pattern, but when there is more than one the spectacle becomes even funnier because they appear to be in competition and race even faster. And they play and butt one another. If only they could speak would they say, 'I'm faster than you, or I'm better than you.' Even the donkey has his moments.

As we journey to and from Mass on Sunday mornings, we come across clusters of bright yellow daffodils, with their heads moving in all directions as the breeze catches them. They seem to arrive very quickly; one week there are none, only green leaves, then all that changes and we are all surprised and delighted when, the next week, the flowers appear.

On these occasions if we are travelling to Mass with Dad or Mum, our excitement may tend to get a little out of hand, and Dad would say '*OK. Settle down. You have all learned the poem in school about the daffodils, so just imagine William Wordsworth coming unexpectedly across those daffodils beside the lake, and feeling so inspired by their beauty that he couldn't help writing about them. On such a day as this anybody would be excited, but before one of you gets hurt as you lark about, let's see how much of the poem we can remember. Let's continue walking line abreast and take it in turns to say a line. We could call it a line in a line. I will repeat the poem for you and you must all pay attention because it will soon be your turn.*'

That usually took the wind out of our sails and we had to calm down quickly, some of us hoping to do better than last time. But it is always funny to watch Dad as he recites this poem, his walk changes slightly, he straightens his back and strikes a pose as he gets carried away with the words.

'I wandered lonely as a cloud
That floats on high o'er vales and hills,
When all at once I saw a crowd,
A host, of golden daffodils;
Beside the lake, beneath the trees,
Fluttering and dancing in the breeze.

Continuous as the stars that shine
And twinkle on the milky way,
They stretched in never-ending line
Along the margin of a bay:
Ten thousand saw I at a glance,
Tossing their heads in sprightly dance.

The waves beside them danced, but they
Out-did the sparkling leaves in glee;
A poet could not be but gay,
In such a jocund company!
I gazed—and gazed—but little thought
What wealth the show to me had brought:

For oft, when on my couch I lie
In vacant or in pensive mood,
They flash upon that inward eye
Which is the bliss of solitude;
And then my heart with pleasure fills,
And dances with the daffodils.'

Fancy telling us to calm down, when just now he seems ready to lift off himself. Heavens, I've been so busy watching where I'm going, watching him and trying not to giggle, that I haven't concentrated on the words. Oh never mind he's kind and patient when teaching us to do things. So now, Dad starts off with the first line and then it's Mum's turn, and with some prompting, as we progress line by line, and down the line and by the time Patrick has had his turn we arrive at Church and, as Dad says, with our knees unblemished.

The fact is though as far as I'm concerned, no one has yet decided to have Easter in April every year and we are stuck with March on this occasion. People are saying it has been a long and dreary winter, with more than the usual amount of illness. In our house there is an empty chair and Granddad often looks very sad. I long to comfort him, but Mum says it will take time and we must be patient, and love him. I do that anyway, very dearly. It doesn't help that we are confined to the house so much; giving up for Lent the things we like to eat is much more difficult when you can't spend much time out of doors – away from temptation. But we are allowed to relax our fast on the 17th March as we celebrate the Feast of St. Patrick. Not only is this a festive day but also a National Holiday too. It is treated like a Sunday, but not any ordinary Sunday. St. Patrick is our Patron Saint and weeks beforehand Mum usually buys cards, with his Picture on, to send to relatives overseas.

Of course she can't send a card without enclosing a sprig of Shamrock. I feel that it must be in a sad state when it arrives, but this year Mum has bought some special boxes which she says should keep it in better condition, but we though, won't know for some time if it has been successful. It hadn't been easy finding the Shamrock and little wonder since the ground is so cold. Well, I can't ask anyone to change that date, and it is wonderful to have our usual treats – I suppose that is one advantage of having Easter early – and we will have fulfilled our fast.

This year one of Mum's friends, called Nora, has promised to let us have a goose for Easter Sunday but it will need to be collected on the Saturday. Dad is busy on the farm, and doesn't have time to be involved in domestic problems. Tom and Joe are helping him, and Mum has no option but to ask me, *'Do you think you could manage to collect the goose, I have so much to do here?'*

'Well Mum, I manage to go to school and back by myself and that is about half a mile!'

'Collecting the goose means walking over two and half miles,' Mum replies, *'that's about as far as church and as you manage that on Sundays, I suppose you could go. But you had better take Patrick with you to help you with the weight'.*

I don't know what Mum is worried about, because we walk to church on Sundays without breakfast and that's not a problem. Still, it will be nice to have Patrick's company. Mum is very happy with the arrangement but my little brother is not very keen, and expresses his feelings by saying, *'It's a long walk there and back just for a goose! What will you give me?'* He has the same calculating look as when we are playing cards. I know he would like my special spinning top, but no goose, nor any amount of persuasion would make me part with it, because Granddad took a long time to make it, and it is very special to me. My collection of marbles will have to do. Half an hour later Patrick is six, bright, beautiful marbles the richer, while Mum is in a state of panic, saying, *'If you don't hurry you won't get back before dark, and please don't dawdle on the way or stay too long when you get there.'*

We set out fairly briskly, and apart from a scary moment as we pass the field with the bad-tempered bull, trying not to breathe in case he should hear, we arrive at Nora's house feeling quite pleased with ourselves, even though we have been struggling against the freshening breeze towards the end of the journey.

Nora was expecting someone to turn up for the goose, but exclaims upon opening the door, *'Goodness have you two come by yourselves?'*

'We've had to, because Dad and the boys are on the farm and Mum is too busy to leave the house.'

'Well, we had better get you started back as quickly as possible.'

'We don't mind the strong wind blowing us about; it's fun raising our arms and pretending to flap our wings.' Nora gives me a strange look and says, *'Yes, but it could be too strong for you two, and it is blowing in a lot of heavy clouds. We must hurry, but you can't set out without a hot drink and some cake.'*

We follow her into the kitchen, which is lovely and warm; it has a very big range and we can see the fire burning brightly through the grill. Nora tells us to go and sit on the chairs nearest to it and warm ourselves, while she makes us some hot cocoa. This sounds like heaven, and indeed it is when she puts some fairy cakes on a plate and says, *'Help yourselves.'* Mum has always told us that we must only take one and wait until we are offered a second, but Mum isn't here, and the cakes look too good to leave; besides Patrick has three pockets! Nora has said to help ourselves, and she didn't say that we couldn't take one for the trip back; but perhaps it would be polite to ask all the same. Having eaten our cake and drunk our cocoa, Nora kindly offers us some greaseproof paper to save the mess in Patrick's pockets! So with the goose packed in a strong Hessian bag, we set out each holding a handle.

'I'm not sure how you are going to manage,' Nora says, *'but perhaps, sharing the load, you will be able to cope. Be as quick as you can now and be on your way.'* Because she has been so kind, and as we are feeling warm inside and outside, we laugh and thank her, stepping out into the wind.

We weren't to know before we left home that a normal sized goose is about four times heavier than your average duck or chicken, and it isn't long before Patrick says, *'My arm is aching!'* Mine is feeling a bit strange too, and I suggest that we change places and use the other arm. This works quite well at first, but with each swap-over, we realise that both arms are aching, and Patrick is not at all happy. I suggest carrying the bird myself, and pick it up with both arms, but not for long and we have to share the weight again. Sometimes, in a crisis situation we have to play a happy game to get us through, so I say to Patrick, *'Imagine we have wings and when we get to the top of the hill we can fly all the way home.'* Unfortunately the top of the hill is not appearing as fast as we would like. We are walking into the wind now, and it is becoming much stronger, and the first rain drops have started. It's only light drizzle at the moment, but what a pity the wind isn't behind us to push us and our baggage along.

Eventually we arrive at the crossroads, with very tall, overhanging trees on both sides; and the dark shadow of the castle rising even higher still. It was this stretch that people would talk about when they were referring to the banshee, and you certainly wouldn't want to be there after dark. Patrick and I seem to have one and the same thought, throw caution to the wind, and leave the dead goose to whoever might find it. Although we aren't far from home now, we might as well be on the far side of the moon, because nobody likes going through the crossroads especially at night time.

I am remembering occasions when we have taken our fears to our parents, and after reassuring words they have reminded us that a little fear is not a bad thing; it can help us sometimes to avoid making silly mistakes and at other times help us to be brave. It was easy to be guided by their wisdom, but how I wish one of them could be here now. I know Patrick is just as petrified, because he has started shaking and when he whispers his teeth are chattering, which does nothing whatsoever to reassure me.

It is raining steadily now, and the trees, which in the summer cause one big shadow, now look so menacing as they tower over us. They look like a forest of evil beings, with thick twisted bodies and lots of arms, just waiting to reach out and grab us, and no happy game is going to help us here. The wild thought about leaving the goose doesn't help either, although for a moment I feel that if we had a live, struggling, gaggling goose in the bag it would have been more reassuring, because at least it would have been real! Well, it isn't alive and we are rooted in fear. Patrick starts to cry, and I am fast losing my determination to be a proper big sister. Oh my Lord, what else have we been told to do? Oh yes, of course, I remember, Mum says, *'When all else fails you must say a prayer.'* Well, I prayed to my invisible friend when the bull was chasing Dad and he escaped just in time. Now, perhaps I could pray and ask Him to send our Guardian Angels, and I will ask Patrick to pray too. And so we say a prayer together; we recite all the prayers that we have learned and end with a whispered, 'Please help us Lord.'

As so often happens here on wet wintry afternoons, the light goes very quickly, and it becomes pitch black in no time at all. Dad has hurried home with the boys and Mum has told him about our excursion. He collects the big lantern from the shed and sets out to find us. The crossroads are not far from our house, but we can no longer see the road. Nevertheless we consider shuffling along, as the stones underfoot will hopefully guide us, and we could even try dragging the goose. We are just about to move, when we are suddenly fixed to the spot again, because we can see a light coming towards us. Oh, it is all too much! Who wants to be brave when Jack-o-the-Lantern appears. Dropping the goose we clutch each other for comfort, standing stock still, with eyes tight shut and pray it will not notice us and pass us by quickly. Then we hear a very calm voice say, *'Thank God you're safe,'* and we open our eyes to see Dad's smiling face above the lantern. Patrick and I whisper through chattering teeth, *'And we thank God too.'*

Dad leads the way home with the lantern and the goose, while we – still holding hands – silently follow, walking in the arc of the light.

CHAPTER 17
THE RAINBOW AND THE PROMISE

Christmas has come and gone, and in January Grandma has left us too. For a time life is subdued and we have had our minor ailments. The weather, which is at its bleakest at this time of year, makes it difficult to be out of doors. On occasions the snow has been too deep for us to attempt going to Church or School. Finding quiet pastimes for four boisterous youngsters can be a real problem for our parents, but Mum doesn't waste an opportunity and quietly asks Granddad if he can set us some homework. This used to be one of Grandma's favourite duties, but I think Mum feels that it might cheer him up. She is so right! Not only does he rise to the challenge, he also manages to introduce another challenge, by way of a bribe, *'One shilling for the first one to complete the exercise book!'* This is not really the sort of challenge which my brothers want to have, since it will use up the time they need to set the traps to catch birds, something that they would much rather be doing. Of course, they release the birds immediately because we are not going to have blackbirds in a pie for tea – not four and twenty of them anyway! Their particular challenge is the excitement of who can catch the most, but it does allow us the opportunity of having a closer look at them before we let them go.

Even though the ground has been covered in snow, or merely frozen, it is still possible to look down the hill to the sea below, which is reflecting the clouds and the sky – all shades of grey. These times are often shared with Granddad now, who has more time on his hands these days and loves to chat, but he seems more inclined to talk about the greyness of the sky and the clouds, reflecting on his own life, the greyness and the sadness since Grandma is not around. I long to remind him that he once told me, even though the sky may be grey and thick with clouds, the sun is shining above and will break through eventually, if we are patient and wait long enough. Well, I will be patient but I hope that there will soon be a sign, which will help him to feel happier. We don't have long to wait, because instead of working on my exercise book, I look through the window at the clouds and he says, *'There is a storm brewing, but perhaps it will clear the air.'* The storm does come, but quickly passes, and we can see the winter sun peering through the clouds. It is then that it happens, and my prayers are answered. There it is, very faint at first and far out over the sea - a rainbow, a sign of hope, a promise that soon everything will be better. As we look through the kitchen window, I steal a glance at Granddad and feel that some of the sadness has gone. I ask if it is true, does a leprechaun sit under the rainbow hammering away as he makes his shoes? And Granddad replies, *'No one knows but it is said that the person who finds the leprechaun will also find the pot of gold. No one has ever proved it but people go on hoping just the same.'*

I started to giggle, while he was still talking, because I know this story very well and have been thinking ahead:

'Well Granddad, I would love to find the leprechaun, and I love the rainbow too; it has all my favourite colours, but there is no way that I want to chase it across the sea.'

At this his sense of humour returns and he laughingly says, *' Oh I see, you don't want to be like Niamh on her beautiful white horse?'*

'Oh Granddad, my favourite story! Will you tell it to me again?'

'Fionn Mac Cumhail was a very brave Celtic warrior, who had a son called Oisín. Now, Oisín was not only a brave warrior, but he also loved to sing, recite poetry and play the harp. By the time he was twenty years of age, he was so well known throughout the land, that people came from every province to hear him recite poems, sing or play the harp.

One day Oisín was out hunting with his father, near the shores of a lake, when a beautiful maiden approached them, riding on a magnificent snow-white horse. She had long golden hair, and her skin was pale and as fresh as early morning dew. Her dress was gossamer silk, and her robe was decorated with jewels of every description, and on her feet she wore golden slippers. Looking at Fionn she cried, "Oh, I have found you at last Fionn Mac Cumhail."

"Yes you have, but who are you and where have you come from?" said Fionn.

"I am Niamh of the Golden Hair," she replied, "and I have come from Tír na nÓg, which is a beautiful land far across the sea, where the sun never sets and no one ever grows old. I have come to find your son Oisín, because I have heard so much about his bravery and eloquence; I wish to take him back with me to Tír na nÓg, where my Father is the King."

Fionn said, "You are most welcome in our land Princess Niamh, and I hope you will spend many a happy day with us!"

The Princess stayed with them for some time, and each day she listened to Oisín reciting his poetry and playing his harp. Gradually they both fell very much in love; then the day dawned when Niamh said to Fionn, "I must return to my own land, for my Father is waiting for me." Turning to Oisín she said,"Will you come with me Oisín?"

He replied, "Yes, I will come with you to your land of Eternal Youth." Fionn was very sad on hearing their news, and knew that he would not see his son again, but Oisín promised that he would return within a year. Leaping on to the back of the horse behind Niamh, he bade his father farewell, as the horse leapt forward to ride back over the waves. Very soon they arrived in Tír na nÓg, where the land was exactly as Niamh had described it; the sea was beautifully blue and clear, the sand was a lovely shade of pale gold, and the grass was even greener than the green grass of home.

The King and Queen were delighted to welcome this brave and eloquent warrior to their family, and quickly arranged for the happy couple to be married. For three hundred years Oisín was content to be with Niamh in this wonderland, but as time went by he began to grieve for his own native land, and he wished to see his Father again. Eventually he even lost his desire to sing, but when he told Niamh about his feelings she said, "I fear that if you go I will never see you again." But he promised that he would not stay long, and would soon be back with her again. As she saddled her beautiful horse, she said, "Go if you must, but please be very careful for if your foot touches Irish soil you will never return again to this land!" She bade him a sad farewell, and soon the horse was galloping over the waves back to the land of his Father. But when he arrived nothing was the same, as everything had changed. The land looked different and his Father's fortress lay in ruins, covered in brambles, briars and ivy. He was distraught, but when he asked about his own people, he was told that they had been long since gone.

Oisín felt a desperate sadness in his heart, and turned the horse to head back to Tír na nÓg, but as he did so, he noticed some men who were trying to move a large stone. Not understanding their size and weakness, since he was so big and strong, he offered to help them. Leaning down from the saddle, he prepared to move the stone with one arm, but as he did so, the saddle girth broke and he fell to the ground. In an instant he changed from being a brave young warrior to a very withered old man. The horse became frightened and took off at a gallop, and headed back to Tír na nÓg. The men were also frightened and wished to help the old man. Oisín explained who he was, and who his Father had been – a fighting warrior. When they heard this, they told him about St. Patrick, and how he had changed their fighting ways. They took Oisín to see St. Patrick, who listened in wonder to his story, and he asked his monks to write it all down, so that the story didn't become lost with the passing of time. Oisín was converted by St. Patrick and died very soon afterwards.'

As we continue to gaze at the rainbow, I try to imagine being in Tír na nÓg; feeling the warmth of the sun, admiring the beautiful scenery, but most of all listening to the magical sounds coming from the harp. Oh how wonderful to be in a place where time stands still, but as I return to reality I know that I don't want things to remain as they are now, because I don't like being in doors for so much of the time and so I am waiting patiently for spring to arrive.

'Granddad, nobody mentioned the rainbow last summer when we were talking about the Celts, but they would have seen it wouldn't they?'

'Oh yes, they would have appreciated the glorious colours, and we did tell you that they had a reverence for all these things, but we also told you that they didn't understand just how everything came to be. Their means of interpreting beauty was very different from ours. I think they would have had a clear understanding of the clouds though; the bright silver ones and the dark, dark grey ones, but it was probably the pale clouds and the sun setting in the west which inspired them most.

You know everyone needs to express their sense of beauty, whether it is in a calm manner or, as some people do, in a noisy exciting way, as you sometimes do when you want to skip and dance or sing. We can speculate that the Celts felt very deeply about poetry, music and art, and this could have been a means of expressing their inner beauty too. As you just heard in the story about Tír na nÓg, they invented other worlds where the living go on living forever, and even the spirits of the dead go on living too.'

'I love the fairy stories Granddad, and it's so exciting to see the shapes and colours of the clouds, especially when the sun shines on them; it is so magical looking at the sea too, as the moving clouds cast their shadows on the water, making it look deeper as the colour changes. But looking at the rainbow is so, so different, because whether it is clear and sharp, or just hazy the colours blend so softly and mysteriously. It makes me glow inside. Do you think I could paint it when I grow up?

'Well, anyone can paint a rainbow, but to get the fusion of colour, as you see it in the sky, needs a very special talent or gift; what really matters now, and in the future, is not whether you can paint it, but how it makes you feel inside. Knowing you as I do, I believe that the beauty that you see all about you will always be reflected within you, because you allow yourself to see it with your mind and heart.'

'Can't everyone do that?'

'Yes they can if they allow themselves to, except perhaps those who have no vision, but I am sure even those people wish they were able to. Now though the rainbow is fading, and while it is still there I need to tell you a little more about it.

The simplest way to explain would be to start with one of our cut crystal glasses, which we use occasionally. If the sun is shining when Mum next washes them, ask her to hold one of them up in the sun's rays while the glass is still wet. You will see it sparkle with all the colours of the rainbow, because the light reflects through the water droplets. These drops are round and act like prisms catching the light. The cut crystal also catches the light even when dry, and it is possible to see these colours when turning the glass slowly. Clouds are made up of millions of water droplets, and a rainbow is caused when some of these are falling through the air, usually towards the end of a shower of rain. It can be seen in the sky opposite to the sun's direction. The sunlight enters the rain droplets and becomes bent and reflected. The white light breaks up into the colours of the spectrum through a prism effect of the water droplets, rather like the effect on the crystal, which I mentioned earlier. The rainbow is higher in the sky when the sun is low, but a point is reached when the sun is too high in the sky for the rainbow to be seen at all.'

'I think I understand most of that Granddad, but it wouldn't make me want to paint it as I see it now. Are there any poems about the rainbow, like the skylark poem and the daffodil poem? Maybe, if I'm not clever enough to paint it, I could write about it!'

'You know, my dear, I wouldn't worry about any of that right now, just be as you are. I have been talking to you about science, and to the best of my knowledge there aren't any poems or odes to the rainbow, but that could be because poets cannot find the right words to describe what they see. But the rainbow has a very special meaning for us, because of what we read in the Bible in the Genesis story. Do you remember the Great Flood, when God was so angry because the people wouldn't listen to him?'

Oh dear, I felt I had to explain to him now that the old Bible stories made me feel quite bad inside, and I preferred the new ones about Jesus. He patiently explains that it was because of what happened in the old stories that God needed to send his Son to show us how we should behave if we really wanted peace on earth and happiness in eternity.

'Oh Granddad, I'm sorry, and I promise to listen more carefully to the old stories from now on.'

'Now, my dear, that word promise is the best word you could have chosen to use, because that's what the rainbow means to us. We will read the story of the flood together sometime, but our rainbow has almost gone. Each time you see it from now on, you will remember that God promised that he would never again send a flood. He said, "Whenever I cover the sky with clouds and the rainbow appears, I will remember my promise to you, and to all the animals, that a flood will never again destroy all living beings." And our rainbow has now gone.'

'Granddad, do you think that God is trying to remind us of the power that only He has, as well as His promise?'

'Oh my little one, what a lot of questions!'

'O Joy that seekest me through pain,
I cannot close my heart to thee;
I trace the rainbow through the rain,
And feel the promise is not vain,
That morn shall tearless be.'

The Robin

Once I loved a robin redbreast, it shard my home with me,
We also shared at breakfast time our butter, toast and tea.
Springtime came, it built its nest quite near my kitchen door;
Soon three baby robins picked breadcrumbs from the floor.

All summer long it sang its song from a sheltered sycamore tree,
Blue-winged flies and midges it gobbled with unholy glee.
When other birds are silent, in autumns shortening days,
My robin sang as sweetly as in the sun's bright rays.

Winter came with frost and snow, as time sped swiftly on,
It came and went, I asked no rent, save the joy it gave in song.
But illness came upon me, and I was forced to go,
To leave my little redbreast friend, to battle with the foe.

I tell a doleful story, my heart is sad and sore,
For I know my little redbreast friend flits vainly by the door.
I will ask the God of sparrows, who looks after robins too,
To find some friendly doorway, where breadcrumbs are not few.

And when little bright eyes are closing, as close will also mine,
We'll wing our flight to heaven, to praise the Lord Divine.

Catherine Clancy 15th March 1988

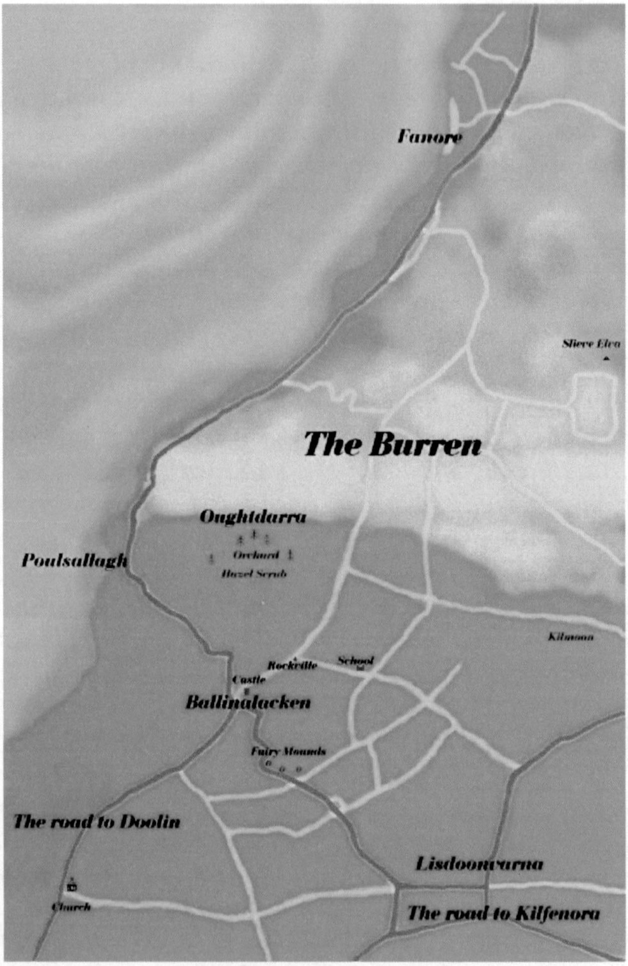

Map of the Burren

By the Fireside

View from Rockville down to the sea at Doolin.

Why am I here and is this where I belong

The Burren is famous for its wild flowers, and this is where I belong.

The Box Camera

Rockville and the 'T' Junction.

<u>The Meadow and The Church</u>

Holy Rosary Church at Doolin.

The Peat Bog

Every farm had its donkey, as indeed they do today.

Going Hunting

View from High Road near Rockville
with Doolin in the far distance.

The Pig

'The word usually spreads – not that words are necessary because I think the squeals will have been heard over a wide distance.'

As The Crow Flies

The incredible landscape of the Burren, unchanged over the centuries, and showing one of the more significant 'erratics'.

Summer Drives to Kilfenora

My son Alan, by the grave of his great-great-uncle, at Kilfenora Cathedral.

The Cathedral and the Celts

Celtic High Cross in the field near Kilfenora Cathedral.

Who Were The Celts

Nature – a living, breathing, creation story.
The cliffs where the Burren meets the sea.

Origins Of The Celts

'The land speaks of higher, holier things ...'
The Portal Tomb at Poulnabrone.

Creativity and the Celts

Waves at Doolin create unusual scenes. This shows the contrast between the foam in the foreground and the surf beyond.

The Cathedral And The Legacy

The Rock of Cashel, where St. Patrick famously converted the Celtic King.

Hazel Nuts

The dense hazel grove with nuts ripe for picking.

The Funeral

The sun setting over Doolin,
as viewed from Rockville.

The Goose

The road home with the goose passes
beneath Ballinalacken Castle.

The Rainbow and The Promise

'Well Granddad, I would love to find the leprechaun,
and I love the rainbow too; it has all my favourite colours,
but there is no way that I want to chase it across the sea.'